THE DEEP END OF THE OCEAN

It's the moment every mother dreads — three-year-old Ben is gone, and no one can find him. Despite a police search that will turn into a nation-wide obsession, Ben has vanished, seemingly without a trace. His disappearance will leave Beth frozen on a knife-edge of suppressed agony for nine years and drive a shattering wedge through her marriage to Pat. Then something so unexpected happens, it changes everything that once seemed true or possible. And perhaps, only perhaps, it will give Beth what she thought was gone forever: a reason to live.

JACQUELYN MITCHARD

THE DEEP END OF THE OCEAN

Complete and Unabridged

NIAGARA

Ulverscroft Group Limited

England - USA - Canada

Australia - New Zealand

First published in the
United States of America

First Niagara Edition
published 1996

Published in Large Print
by arrangement with
Viking Penguin
New York

ISBN 0–7089–5848–6

ULVERSCROFT
Large Print

Published by
F. A. Thorpe (Publishing) Ltd.
Anstey, Leicestershire

Set by Words & Graphics Ltd.
Anstey, Leicestershire
Printed and bound in Great Britain by
T. J. Press (Padstow) Ltd., Padstow, Cornwall

This book is printed on acid-free paper

For the two Dans,
and for my father and my mother

Acknowledgments

Though there usually turns out to be only one name on the cover, every book's a collaborative effort, and that is monumentally true for this one.

Without the support and encouragement of key angels in my life, it would still be, as it was for two years, four pages on a forgotten disc at the back of a drawer. For getting it out of the drawer, I must first thank the two Janes, my friend Jane Hamilton and my friend and agent, Jane Gelfman, one who said I could do this, the other who said I had.

I also wish to extend my deepest gratitude and affection to the Ragdale Foundation on Lake Forest, Illinois, where substantial portions of this book were written in 1994 and 1995, especially to Annie Adams and Sylvia Brown. For their expertise, I want to thank police officers Nancy Robinson, Mary Otterson, and Ralph Gehrke; medical specialists Marilyn Chohaney and Tom O'Connor; David Collins of the Matthew Collins Foundation for Missing Children; lawyers Michele La Vigne and Kaye Schultz; and for special valor, my basketball tutors — Rick, Mike, and T. And for their astonishing faith in me, to Barbara Grossman and Pam Dorman, thank you.

For their endurance and generosity, Hannah Rosenthal and Rick Phelps, Jean Marie and

Christian Kammer, Georgia Blanchfield and John Wiley, Steve Schumacher and Victoria Vollrath, Franny Van Nevel and the rest of my Madison circle deserve a medal of honor, as do my friends from afar — especially my dear Joanne Weintraub, and also Bridget Flanner Forsythe, Deborah Toscano, Anne D. LeClaire and Kobena Eyi Acquah.

Most urgently, let me thank my family for their tolerance in sharing my heart and mind for so long.

To my son Robert, who is my right arm and sometimes my left, and to my sunshine son, Daniel, and my son Martin, the small Hemingway who titled this book, and to the beautiful woman who is my daughter, Jocelyn, and to my daughter of the heart, Christin, bless you for staying the course. When I promised that this was as much for you as for me, I meant it; and I love you beyond reckoning.

Madison, Wisconsin
June 3, 1995

Grief fills up the room of my absent child,
Lies in his bed, walks up and down with me,
Puts on his pretty looks, repeats his words,
Remembers me of all his gracious parts,
Stuffs out his vacant garments with his form.
Then I have reason to be fond of grief.
Fare you well. Had you such a loss as I,
I could give better comfort than you do.

King John, Act III, scene iv,
by William Shakespeare

Prologue

November 1995

ALTOGETHER, it was ten years, easily ten, from the hot August morning when Beth put the envelope full of pictures into the drawer until the cold fall afternoon when she took them out and laid them one by one on her desk.

Ten years and change, actually. The summer just past had marked a full year since Beth had learned what happened to her son Ben. And if she counted the whole spiraling spectacle of what came after, it was really closer to eleven. Just weeks before, in October, a front-page story called 'Ben: An Epilogue' had appeared in *USA Today* — a belated 'one year later' attempt based on a couple of stale quotes from those few people who would still talk to the press. But it hadn't been the story that reminded Beth of the pictures.

She had simply awakened one morning knowing. She would look.

It was raining that day, a chill, insistent November murk. For years, rain had frightened Beth into a concentrated burst of the most habitual quotidian tasks. But, that day, even the rain did not dissuade her. She was, if anything, in a hurry, as if looking at the pictures would put a period at the end of a sentence that had straggled all over the page.

Beth laid the pictures out, only sixteen — a small roll, because Pat had used that silly little Instamatic then, the one that embarrassed Beth. She laid them facedown, like an old lady laying solitaire in a window seat.

And then she closed her eyes and touched one.

It did not vibrate. There was no voltage. All she felt was Kodak paper, feathery with a skin of dust. Nothing mystical. Beth caught her breath in relief. All those years. The seal had remained tight, like closed paper lips, with the date stamped across it in smeared ink, an astounding prophecy. June third, and the year. June third, a Saturday, because Pat had dropped the roll off at the mall color booth the day she left for the reunion. When he remembered to pick them up, at the end of that erased first summer, Pat had come into the house sobbing and given them to Beth, as if expecting she would enfold him, comfort him by somehow managing to cope with the evidence.

Instead, she had taken the picture folder securely between two flat hands and brought it to her desk. It had seemed important then — she had never been exactly certain why — that she always knew where the pictures were, no matter how uncomfortable that sometimes was. For example, there were the times Beth glimpsed the envelope when she opened her desk drawer to reach for her paper clips or her address stamp. She did it quickly, as she once used to gather her speed before rushing past the

Goya print of Kronos munching on a child that her grandmother Kerry unaccountably kept on a wall at the turn of the stairway. She felt the same oxygen deficit when she closed the drawer as she did when she put that hideous image behind her.

But she still sometimes saw it, and once or twice she actually brushed the envelope with her fingers. And when they'd been packing for their move to Chicago, Beth had gone purposefully to the drawer as if she actually meant to take those pictures out and look at them.

But she hadn't. It had still been too soon. Too soon to look, too soon to toss.

There were other things left over from Ben that Beth had gradually found the nerve to give away or pack up. On a few rainy days, suffocating days, she had even broken some of those things — a music box, a ceramic picture frame decorated with nursery blocks.

She had never even considered doing that with the pictures. After all, Beth was a photographer; pictures were talismans to her. But she also had a sense that a time might come when she could cherish those photos, particularly the last one on the roll, the porch snapshot. The simple passage of time, or religion, or resignation, might make it her bittersweet delight, a record of Ben the last time she saw him — well, not the last time she saw him, but the last time she saw him as he was, her sunny, uncomplex son, the one who never came to her dreams, though she bade him often, weeping, thinking that at least she need not fear him in her sleep. And

3

so someday, perhaps when she was dying and was sure that frank oblivion was her immediate prospect, when she was sure that she was not going to have to drag herself through more life, she might want to look at those pictures often, perhaps every day.

So she'd need them handy. Otherwise, she'd lose them. That became especially clear when she returned home, weeks after the reunion, and noticed how she had begun to lose everything with remarkable ease, how keys, checks, paper money floated from her hands as if they had their own kinetic lives. Beth would stand in her kitchen unable to remember, as she unpacked a grocery bag or folded laundry, where cereal went and where sheets. She learned to regard it as chronic, like a limp after an accident.

It was only when she looked back at its progress that Beth could see her impairment was a deliberate choice, not a temporary fog that could have burned off when she felt equal to seeing things clearly. The impairment was her training. She taught herself to veer off, mentally, into the tall grass of lost school forms and stuffed peppers, at the first hint that a memory of Ben, or of that day, was about to break the surface.

Beth knew that she could not bear up under those thoughts; and she could not heal without inviting them. And so she had made the choice, it seemed now, to not heal. Instead, she would try to live around the friable edges of a crater, to tread softly and avoid what she had come to think of as the avalanche.

Without success, Beth had tried to explain the

4

avalanche and the necessity of confounding it to her husband, Pat.

She'd tried and sounded like a fool, telling him about people who had a disease — Korsakov's syndrome — that sliced their memory to moments. Such patients, mostly alcoholics, could meet a doctor, a social worker and talk intelligently for long minutes, about the weather, their health, the stories on the front page of a newspaper spread on a desk. But should the doctor or the social worker leave the room, even for a minute, victims of Korsakov's would have no memory of ever having met any such person. Introductions would begin all over again.

That, Beth told her husband, was nearly how she felt — how, in fact, she longed to feel. A virtually functional woman, who would look normal to anyone who couldn't see the key in her back. But Pat, who had watched her become a robot wife and mother, thought her grief irrational. Pat grieved for Ben as a normal person would grieve, as if they'd lost their little boy to childhood cancer or a wildfire outbreak of some outmoded disease, polio or diphtheria. As time passed, Pat proceeded through grief's 'stages', almost in the manner described in Compassionate Circle pamphlets.

Beth couldn't do that. It seemed to her a process as impossible as cutting your straight hair short and willing it to grow out curly.

What she felt about Ben, Beth tried to tell Pat, was as similar to that sort of grief as a biplane is similar to a dragonfly.

Grief, Beth knew. When Beth was eighteen, her mother had died, of a complex series of organ failures and cluster catastrophes that started with a kidney cyst, hurtling toward death with an absurd speed that ended the day she was brought home in an ambulance after breakfast only to leave again in a hearse after dinner. It had been horrible, a train wreck, a blunt invasion of Beth's life.

But it wasn't her fault.

Beth had not teased a pestilent growth out of her mother's kidney. Nothing she neglected to give or do or say had drifted off her like contagion and settled on her mother.

Losing her mother had been regular old agony, not a trip to the lip of the avalanche. If she dared to embrace what she really felt about Ben's loss — pulled apart the skeins of stupidity and lack and the truth that everything that matters in life is decided irrevocably in seconds — Beth knew something would happen to her. And it was that, the beyond-grief, the sealing-up of a mind still expected to produce order and plans, which she dreaded.

She'd had little tastes of it, small rock slides that caught her unawares, sending her from room to room, bent over, panic rumbled over longing. Images of him in a closet, or a grave. The churn of her bowels as her brain popped his name. His one-bell Ben name.

And then, unless someone, someone persuasive, Ellen or Candy, was there to redirect her, Beth would begin, feverishly, to rewrite the rest of that day, restring the entrances and exits, and all the elements of plot, revamp the dialogue as if she were an artist who could fill in speech balloons from people's mouths. All the while, above her, ominous rumbles, glacial shifts. Beth would shuffle faster, irresistibly trying to imagine a way to beg back ten minutes, maybe four minutes, long enough to walk back over to the luggage trolley, where Vincent stood, whining and fidgeting, and take Ben back to the hotel registration counter with her. Or perhaps even let the panicky, dropping moments happen, if they had to, for the sake of penance, but then let the tape play in reverse, fast, and see Ben come walking to her, backwards, from the magazine stand or the revolving door, or wherever he had first gone — theories varied. Come walking back and back into her, into her arms, his overround belly pulsing against her hands, his heart beating as it did when he was scared or startled — beating so she could almost feel the outline of it, like Road Runner's in the cartoon, after he outsmarted the coyote Ben, smelling of red pop and Irish Spring, and if he was hot, a little tang, like the smell of rubber bike handles, because he was too young to truly have hormones. She would feel herself spanking him; she would have spanked him, she would admit to herself, during those rock slides, just once, hard, felt his threadbare favorite denim shorts under her hand. Feel his cupped little rear, so firmly packed it seemed he had water injected just under his skin.

Feel Ben. Ben safe.

It was that palpable sense of presence shoved

up against the reality of absence, like hot against cold, that really threatened to buckle the whole mass. Then Beth would have to strain to stop it.

What resulted looked like stoic calm, to editors she worked with, sometimes even to family. And indeed, Beth appreciated that her impairment, like courage, was a state of grace. But only she understood the disadvantages. She knew that for a very long time she had not actually 'loved' the children, though she was careful to be mostly kind and sometimes noticing to them. She was certain that Kerry especially, who had never known Beth any other way, didn't feel the difference.

But Vincent did. Especially on those nights when Beth, on the way to school to pick him up, would forget where she was and why. When she'd finally arrive, sweating, Vincent would be standing outside the school, bouncing his basketball in the gathering darkness, looking at her with a scorn so bold that had she been able to feel anything at all about him, she would have been enraged.

On the whole, however, it worked. What, after all, had she given up to protect herself and her remaining children from abuse, or worse? The odd few years of examined life?

A more-than-fair trade.

So, when she turned over the first photograph — even in the full knowledge that the images could no longer hold any dread — she still felt that minute tectonic shift, and the impulse to run from the landslide.

When she fought that impulse down, Beth recognized, all in a wave, what she had really been seeking from the pictures, especially the last one, taken just as they set off for the reunion. The real reason she'd been unwilling to discard them.

She realized what she was looking for, and that it wasn't there.

Not in any of them — not in the picture of Vincent fishing at Terriadne, or of Ben feeding Kerry her bottle. Especially in the porch picture, the worst shot on the roll, intended, really, only to capture Pat's lilacs. She and the children were just a prop for the record of Pat's horticultural triumph. Even so, it had taken forever. Beth recalled her husband scolding Vincent for fidgeting.

But in fact, Beth saw now, it was Ben who had moved.

She wouldn't have recognized him. Beth had not seen her son's three-year-old image for a very long time by then, and in a real sense it was the image of a child she'd never really known. Not her baby Ben. A little-boy Ben she'd only just met.

She stared at the picture, wishing she had her good photographer's loupe. There was Jill, Pat's nineteen-year-old cousin, who lived with them then and helped out while she went to school, carrying Beth's cameras and bags. Jill with long hair, looking like a sunny little hippie. There was Kerry, a minuscule infant face above a dress bordered with red and blue and yellow boats. Vincent had still been blond. Beth could not remember her older son, with his brown mat, lush and coarse as bear fur, ever having been blond.

But Ben's face, that was a blur.

Poised to receive that face like sacrament from the drawer bottom, she saw instead . . . not much of anything. She saw details — how very many freckles he'd had on his arms, how long and enormously well-muscled his legs were, even as a preschooler. But his face . . . all you could tell was that his mouth was open. He had been talking. But his features were indistinct. There was no message. Even changed as she now was, on the molecular level — all her old beliefs discarded — she realized that she had still, somehow, expected it.

Beth had been a newspaper photographer and photo editor, working mostly freelance, since college. When she edited, because of the nature of what scholars wrote about, Beth got to see many photos of people who later came to trouble. Soldiers in fresh uniforms with raw shaves. Immigrant families at the metal rails of ships, in layers of clothes, their luggage beside them on the deck. Cowboys. Aviators.

She thought sometimes that in those muddy images she saw a hint, a foreknowledge, of the mishap to come. The clue, she fancied, was the look in people's faces. A vulnerability? A message of departure in the photo grain? To test her theory, she once showed a picture to Pat, an old picture of a sailboat pilot who drowned on a routine pleasure voyage on a

10

good bright day, after a spectacular career. She'd asked Pat, "Can't you see that man is doomed?"

And Pat patiently explained to her that she was crazy, that no one ever had a presentiment of tragedy until after it occurred; those stories of precognition were balm for weak minds, stuff his aunt Angela, widowed from birth, would say if a baby was born breech, or the phone rang twice and stopped. "Could you see in Abraham Lincoln's face as a young lawyer that he was going to be president? That he was going to be murdered?"

"Yes," said Beth, then. "I could."

"Could you see in the newspaper picture of that kid Eric's face, that kid my sister had in her music class, that he was going to be crushed under a semi on the way to graduation?"

"Absolutely," she told him, wondering how Pat could have missed it. But Pat just sighed, and called her 'the bleak Irish,' the in-home disaster barometer, ready to plummet at a moment's notice.

But Beth had once put stock in such things. Signs and portents, like water going counterclockwise down a sink drain before an earthquake. When she was seventeen, she believed that missing all the red lights between Wolf Road and Mannheim would mean that when she got home her mother would tell her that Nick Palladino had called. She believed, if not in God, then in saints who had at least once been fully human. She had a whole history, a life

11

structure set up on luck, dreams, and hunches.

And it all went down like dominoes in a gust, on the day Ben disappeared.

There had been no warning. There never was any, at all.

Part One

1

Beth

June 1985

"I ONLY like the baby," Beth told her husband, as they stacked plastic bags and diaper bags, and duffel bags and camera bags, and Beth's big old Bacfold reflector — all in a pile in the hall.

She was surprised when Pat looked at her with disgust; she knew he didn't want to fight, didn't want to make trouble on the verge of clearing the whole tribe out for a weekend.

It was foolish in the extreme — her plan to take all the children to Chicago, attend her fifteenth high-school reunion and shoot a job — according to Pat.

But once she insisted, Pat, always happiest solitary, was probably looking forward to a bachelor's forty-eight hours, to sleeping late, to shooting pool at Michkie's, next door to the restaurant, after closing. He didn't dare argue, or Beth would be just as likely to turn around and leave Ben or Vincent behind. Still, the look he gave Beth was ugly, and it never failed to surprise her when he was shocked by the things she said to shock him. "Why?" he finally asked her. "You blurt stuff like that out, you don't mean it, and Vincent could hear you."

15

"I mean it," said Beth. "I really, really mean it." And thought, I don't just torture Pat, I get a kick out of it.

In fact, Vincent did not hear Beth. He was slumped in a corner of the sofa, watching the videotape of *Jaws*, from which Pat had obsessively edited all the bloody footage, his face clenched in what would have been, if he hadn't been seven, and still forgivable, a scowl instead of a pout. He didn't want to go anywhere in the car. He didn't think the idea of going to a hotel and swimming in a big pool with Jill while Mama saw all her old friends sounded like fun. He wanted to stay home and play with Alex Shore; he wanted to go to the restaurant with Daddy. He had told Beth so this morning, eight times.

"You cannot go to the restaurant with Daddy," she finally snapped at him, wondering if she would actually lay hands on him if she heard his wheedling voice just one more time. "Daddy will be working."

"I can sit quiet in the back," Vincent told her stubbornly. "I did it that one time."

It had been the peak experience of Vincent's life thus far — going to spend a Saturday night with Pat at the restaurant he managed for his uncle Augie. He'd been able to go because Beth had the flu, Kerry was just days old, and the last sitter in America was at the prom. The largest thing Beth did with Vincent (she had let him follow her onto a movie set while she shot stills; Paul Newman had shaken his hand), this was nothing to Vincent compared

16

with the fabled night at Cappadora's. His white-haired uncle Augie had carried Vincent around on his shoulders, and Daddy had given Vincent anchovy olives while he sat high on the polished bar.

"Mama was sick then," Beth explained with a patience she did not feel; she hoped, in fact, Vincent could tell how close she was to meltdown. "Mama's well now, and we planned to go all together to Chicago, and you'll see Aunt Ellen, and I need you to help me watch Ben and Kerry."

"I hate Ben and Kerry, and I hate that I have to do everything, and I'm not even going to get dressed." Vincent hurled himself facedown on the sofa, and when Beth tried to raise him, performed his patented dead-weight drag, until she let him drop in the middle of the family-room floor.

Vincent hated his mother. Beth knew it, believed it was because she had waited until he was more than four, old enough to understand the significance of being her one and only love, to have Ben. Vincent liked Ben; he was drawn to Kerry's shell-like smallness; he adored Pat with a ridiculous, loverlike devotion that almost made Beth pity the child. But Beth was sure her older son considered her a food source and an occasional touch for a toy. When she punished him, Vincent looked at Beth in a way that instantly reminded her of what Pat said about house cats: they were miniature predators; if they were big enough, they would eat you. Beth, on the other hand, was drawn to Vincent with an intensity she didn't have to feign. She didn't just want to love him; she wanted to win him. And, Beth thought, he knows that.

Vincent was not forgiving. Ben was. He was delighted to be going out of town with his mother and his brother that morning, as delighted as he would have been to go to the hardware store or sort laundered socks. Ben wasn't just accommodating; he simply expanded, with great good humor and faith, to fill any space you put him in. When Ben was a baby, Beth had actually taken him to a doctor because he smiled and slept with such uninterrupted content. She asked the doctor if Ben could be retarded. The young man, a Russian immigrant, had not mocked her; he had told her, gently, that he supposed the baby could be impaired — anyone could be — but was there a reason for her fears? Did Ben rock, or bang his head against his crib bars — did he seem to be able to hear her, did he look into her eyes?

Beth told the doctor that, no, Ben didn't rock or avoid her eyes. She tried to avoid the doctor's eyes as she told him, "But Ben's so . . . so quiet, and so content," sounding like the ninny she was. "He doesn't scream, even when he's got a dirty diaper, even when he's hungry. He's so patient."

"And your older boy?"

"He was more . . . present." Vincent had been a thin, wakeful, watchful baby, walking at nine months, talking at ten, telling Beth "Me angry" at a year. The doctor smiled at her. Beth still

18

kept the copy of the bill on which the doctor had scrawled his diagnosis: Good baby. Normal.

Ben had remained undemanding and cheerful. Beth could not imagine how from Pat's cynical idealism, his tense bonhomie, and her melancholy had sprung this sun child. Beth didn't love him more than she did Vincent but she had nothing harsh to say to him. Even when Ben was nuts — and he was nuts frequently, like when he'd come to breakfast with a surgical mask on his head like a beret and two sanitary pads wrapped around each bicep, loot from Kerry's birth he'd found stashed under a bathroom sink — Beth could not find it in her to scold him.

Today, as he waited to get into the car, Ben was lying on the hall floor in a dust-dappled shaft of sunlight, using his heels to pedal himself around in a wheel. "I'm underwater," he told her, drunk on the yellow light in his face, as Beowulf, the family dog, leaped sideways to avoid the human pinwheel. He had begged Beth that morning to make what he called 'mommy bread' (actually, it was 'monkey bread', a sort of cinnamon-scented apology for nonbaking mothers that Beth concocted from store dough rolled into pretzel shapes and slathered with whatever sugary spices she could find). But when she told him she was too busy, he didn't whine. He wandered off, always busy, absorbed. "Ben's on a mission," Pat said.

Ben's preschool teacher had once, gently, suggested Beth might have Ben evaluated for hyperactivity. Beth never did. She and Pat thought Ben was simply like one of those dogs

19

you see advertised in the free classifieds: 'Needs room to run'.

But even his charm was wearing thin today: Ben had just decided to take all the medicine and makeup out of Beth's bags and line the bottles up, like toy soldiers, against the door. Now she stepped on a bottle, cracking it, and vitamins exploded everywhere.

"God damn it," she hissed. And when Pat arrived, gracefully, to help her, she had told him the momentary truth: she liked only Kerry, who was unformed, dependent in simple ways, and could barely sit up.

"Just get on the road," Pat told her. "They'll settle down. They'll go to sleep." It was like Pat to think so; the boys hadn't slept in the car since they were two, and Pat still thought a great pair of Levi's cost $15.95. But Beth had the idea that she was old enough for tension to show on her face; and she wanted to be as close to youthfully attractive as it was possible for her to be tonight. So she and Pat dragged everything out to the Volvo, and strapped Kerry and Ben into their car seats, and got Vincent and Ben out again to make sure they went pee and had their toothbrushes, when Pat suddenly remembered he wanted to finish the roll of film from their camping trip.

"I'm not getting out of this car," Beth said. "I'll pull it up in front of the door on the grass, if you want. Or I'll yell for one of the neighbors to pose by the lilacs."

"Come on," Pat urged her, with the kind of sexual growl that reminded her of a gentle yen she hardly ever felt for him — at least not in the same way she had ten years before.

But to acknowledge the fact that Pat had tried to move her, she agreed to get out, despite Vincent now frankly on the verge of tears, and Ben singing one line from 'House of the Rising Sun' at the top of his voice, over and over.

They stood in the bower the lilacs formed. Pat scolded and then snapped; Beth leaped into the driver's seat. She didn't kiss him. She would see him in two days, anyway. In fact, she would see Pat before the sun went down, Beth later recalled — and she had not kissed him then, either, not then or for months afterward, so that the first time she did, their teeth knocked, like junior-high kids', and she noticed, for the first time, that his tongue tasted of coffee — a thing she had never noticed before, during all the years when his tongue was as familiar in her mouth as her own.

The drive down Route 90 to Chicago was never a pleasure, though she and Pat used to have some fun petting in their old Chevy Malibu, years before, coming home from college for Christmas, to families who were speechless with delight that the two of them were in love. These days, it was simply what it was, a stupid, boring, flat-farms-and-then-suburban-sprawl shot for 150 miles. They made the trip often, because most of both their families lived in the Chicago area. Beth and Pat were considered adventurous for living 'up north', in the Madison outpost Pat's uncle had pioneered in 1968.

Pat and Beth had belonged to each other

from her junior year at the University of Wisconsin — and even, in a sense, before, as the children of parents who didn't consider it a holiday unless they played poker together. They'd played with each other at picnics, and in friendship emergencies. They went to each other's first communions, to each other's high-school graduation parties.

But they never really saw each other as gendered until the day they ran into one another on the library mall in Madison, three hours before they fell into bed at Pat's attic dump and missed the next two days of classes.

By then, her junior year and Pat's first year of grad school, Beth was frankly frightened. She had had a miscarriage, at six weeks, while sitting in the waiting room of a clinic preparing to have an abortion. Her last boyfriend had used a telescope to spy on her after she broke up with him. She believed that bad men would fly into town to ask her out. The only sex she'd ever had that was 'good' had been a front-seat interlude with a friend's fiancé. She was working two jobs — waiting tables in the morning, and at night selling china, with stupefying humiliation, door-to-door to perennially engaged sorority girls. She had no money left for senior year, and she was failing two classes. She felt old. She felt used.

She saw Pat.

He was not handsome, not even when he was young. He had a wide, white smile and straight teeth — 'perfect collusion', he called it — but he was short and slight, with unruly curly brown hair and face-saving huge eyes. His shoulders were broad, but his legs were skinny, almost bowed. Pat looked waifish, starving, and was so uncomfortable around people, so eager to please them, that they believed he was the friendliest guy they ever met. Only Beth knew how pure Pat was, how pathologically just. Even when he grew comfortable enough with Beth to know she would stay, and began to enumerate her failures of honesty, tact, and self-discipline, Beth still believed she slept with a sort of knockoff saint.

She was not in awe of her husband — she came to take for granted in Pat everything she admired so lavishly in Ben. But it had been she, not Pat, who had gotten up from that hard bed, more than a dozen years ago, certain they would marry. She knew at last she was safe. The match quickly became family legend: Evie and Bill's only girl, Angelo and Rosie's only son. Beth couldn't help feeling happy for their parents. Pat had gone to college in Madison because his uncle's restaurant was there, and Pat wanted into the business; and so they stayed, marrying in relief after a couple of uncomfortable years of proving they could live together and force their parents to acknowledge it. When she told the judge — another struggle; their parents actually brought a priest to the ceremony in hopes the young people would see reason at the eleventh hour — she promised to honor and cherish Pat, Beth meant it absolutely.

Who would not? Beth thought now, already regretting her cursory farewell, promising herself

23

to phone Pat as soon as she got to the hotel. She knew she was superficially kind and capable of the surface warmth that made even strangers feel included. But Pat, though not happy, was good.

As Beth sat in traffic backed up for three miles around the huge mall at Woodfield, she caught herself wondering if Pat was so tense, so stereotypically the tie-tugging smoker, because he still believed people could be better than they were, that they could measure up if they tried harder. She imagined what Pat would be doing now, alone in the house. He would be trying to impose order on Beth's chaos — checking canisters for the level of staple food supplies, tossing a hundred drawers, putting the screws in bags, carrying the seed packages out to the garage, throwing out the half-empty packs of stale Chiclets. Beth often heard Pat doing this at night, before he came to bed. She had come to associate that rummaging and reorganizing with Italian ancestry, perhaps because her father-in-law, Angelo, did it, too. Too busy all day to attack the details that nagged at them, they puttered, fussily, fretfully, into the small hours. So did her mother-in-law, Rosie, though she was too much aware of disturbing others to rattle about. She folded laundry, reconciled the business accounts, wrote letters to her cousin in Palermo. She was a silent putterer, a busy wraith in a long white robe.

The first Christmas Beth and Pat were married, his parents and Beth's brothers spent two nights in the newlyweds' sordid rented house

24

off Park Street. Beth's brother Ben, called Bick, named Pat's family 'the night stalkers'. They stayed up late, and then they roamed. "Must be because they're Romans," Bick told her.

Beth had not asked Pat to the dance and dinner that would form the centerpiece of her reunion. He knew plenty of her old Immaculata crowd; he had been two classes ahead of her at the same school. He would have been seamlessly cordial to her friends but it would have been such a strain for him that he might have been sick with a cold for a week afterward. He would have drifted mentally to the stacks of history books he read obsessively, underlining good parts with a yellow marker, like a college kid. He would have been bored, thinking of acres of messy drawer space he itched to attack. He would have found the jokes stiff, the laughter forced, the opportunities for telling old stories and dishing old enemies meaningless and cruel.

Beth, on the other hand, couldn't wait.

She turned the car off, while seven cars back a misfit honked his dismay at the delay. She looked into the rearview mirror. Ben had removed ham from the sandwiches Jill had packed and was wiping down the back window.

"Benbo," she told him sharply, "ham is for eating, not washing." Immediately, disgustingly, Ben popped the smeary ham in his mouth. Beth could have stopped him — but how filthy could it be? Ben picked up and ate floor food every day; he sometimes even put his cereal bowl on the floor so he could imitate the dog. Jill would wash the children. The hotel pool would wash them. Beth was not going to snap.

The traffic inched forward, and she started the car. Vincent was by then poking Ben in the neck, relentlessly, probably painfully, with a yellow rubber Indian chief. She could have stopped him; but wouldn't he then have just done something else? Ben was not crying; and there was a certain high-register urgent tone of crying that Beth had come to regard as her cue for interrupting any atrocity. Today, she would ignore all atrocities except those that broke the skin. She inspected her haircut in the mirror — it was new, and appropriately tousled, and she'd rinsed out the gray with henna. Once the logjam moved, they'd be only half an hour from the hotel, which was near her old high school, in Parkside, Illinois.

"Sing 'Comin' Through the Rye', Mom," Ben suddenly called to her now, ignoring Vincent's increasingly violent pokes. How could he do it? Beth wondered; how could Vincent poke Ben, who loved him so? (She thought, guiltily, How could I squeeze Vincent's arm? Or yell at him, nose to nose?) And Beth began hum-singing aimlessly, "'If a body catch a body . . . '"

Ben asked, "Catch a bunny?"

"No, stupid, a buddy! A buddy!" Vincent cried murderously.

Beth closed her eyes and dreamed of tonight — of all the people from the neighborhood she'd see, who would all be wealthier than she, but not so 'creative', nor so good-looking, and certainly

26

not possessed of so many lovely children. Good-looking, thought Beth. I *am* good-looking. Not pretty, but objectively speaking, a solid seven on the scale. When Beth thought about her own appearance, the word that came to her mind was 'square'. She had square shoulders — a cross to her until they became fashionable — and a square chin. (One of her father's favorite dinner-table stories was a recounting of the first time he'd laid eyes on his only daughter and commented, "That baby has the O'Neill jaw. You could use that jaw to miter corners.") Even Beth's hair, when she let it hang of its own considerable weight, was square, and so, to her continuous despair, were her hips. When she was twelve, her pediatrician had crowed cheerfully to Beth's mother that Beth would "pop 'em out one, two, three with that pelvic structure." And even though until Kerry, Beth did indeed hold the indoor record for easy labors, she still couldn't think of Dr. Antonelli's words without feeling as though she'd been genetically programmed to pull carts like a Clydesdale. Beth's own looks could never hold a candle to Ellen's, though Ellen, her childhood best friend, had spent twenty years telling Beth, "No one ever looks at your butt, Bethie. They never get past the bewitching green eyes."

Ah, Ellen. From Beth's point of view, the whole point of this reunion weekend was Ellen. Ellen was six inches taller than Beth, and thirty pounds heavier, the kind of stacked-up strawberry blonde who still caused men to bump into pillars at the airport.

27

She was waiting for Beth at the hotel. Ellen, who lived in the same westside neighborhood where all of them had grown up, a street over from the house Beth's father still owned, had booked a room for the two of them and a room for Jill and all the kids. She'd left her husband, her son, and a thawed tuna casserole up at her northern-suburban mini-mansion and bought a fancy black rayon dress. She'd sent Beth a drawing of it in the mail. The prospect of the weekend had reduced both of them to seventeen: 'I think if Nick asks us to sit with them, we should,' Ellen wrote on the bottom of the drawing. 'His wife won't mind — after all, you fixed them up.'

Beth's first love, the most beautiful boy she had ever seen, before or since, the memory of whom could still make her abdomen contract, often ran into Ellen and her brothers, and occasionally worked with Ellen's husband on development contracts. Beth had not seen Nick for ten years; they had met last at the funeral of a mutual friend, a boy who'd gone to Vietnam twice and later committed suicide by driving his car into the path of an oncoming freight train. Under the circumstances, though Beth still longed for Nick, thought of him in a syrupy way that had nothing to do with her real life, they had only touched cheeks near the casket. And Beth had wondered then, as she often did, if she should have married him.

Nick Palladino had long been a tough, no student, the kind of kid who seemed headed for life as a knockout shoe salesman who pumped iron and dated Bunnies from the Playboy Mansion downtown. But ten years later, Beth was a newspaper photographer who could barely afford cigarettes, and Nick owned his own business. Fifteen years later, Beth was a magazine photographer who no longer smoked, and Nick had sold his construction firm for more than it would have cost to buy Beth's whole neighborhood in Madison. He was married to Trisha, his cool, slight homecoming-princess wife, who had lived across the hall from Beth at college. On that floor in Kale Hall, Beth used to write to Ellen, she felt marooned on the planet of the Nordic blondes. And Ellen had written back that no matter what happened, Nick would never love anyone else, that he would forgive Beth anything if she'd go back with him.

In her car, Beth hummed, and remembered Trisha.

Trisha was from Maine, and she had never seen anything like the street feast of Our Lady of Mount Carmel. Pat and Beth took Trisha to the parade, during which supplicants carried the figure of the Madonna, covered with ten- and twenty-dollar bills affixed to her ceramic robes, through the streets. They bought Trisha a paper cup of cold lupini beans and stood with her next to the bandstand, where Beth suddenly sensed Nick before she ever saw him. He'd had on the most beautiful coat, leather the color of honey; and he danced with Beth first, while Pat stood by, radiating tolerance, his ring on Beth's finger. And then he danced with Trisha; he was a good dancer. Beth was sick with envy;

they didn't make caramel-haired, light-wristed girls like Trisha on the west side of Chicago. After an hour, there was no turning back. When Trisha married Nick, Beth stood up in the wedding, got drunk, and threw up on her beige organdy dress.

"'Everybody has somebody — nay, they say, have I . . . ,'" Beth sang, swerving across three lanes to head into the home stretch of Interstate 290.

"I love that part," said Ben.

"I hate that part," said Vincent. "Actually, I hate the whole song."

She would not throw up anymore, but Beth wanted to get drunk with Ellen, get drunk and giggle and whisper and rush to the bathroom as if they had important things to conference about in there. She wanted to forget until Sunday that she had had children and a recent Cesarean scar.

Beth had weaned Kerry, though she hated to give her last, least one such short shrift, for the reunion. She'd had her ragged nails shaped and lacquered. Shaved an inch off those square hips with leg lifts.

By the time Beth had eased the wagon under the portico of the Tremont Hotel on School Drive, Ellen was on her, tugging her shoulders, trilling, "You're here! You're here!"

"You will not believe it," Ellen whispered now. "Diane Lundgren is here, and she must go three hundred pounds. I'm serious."

"Who else? Who else?" Beth cried, easing Kerry out of her car seat. But Ellen was by then

30

all over the baby, offering Kerry her necklace of silver filigree balls to chew, sniffing the crown of Kerry's head.

"I'm your godmama, Kerry Rose Cappadora," Ellen cooed, reaching out a hand to each of the boys in turn, pulling them to her with her strong arms and soundly kissing them. The boys, who had grown up believing they were her nephews, didn't struggle; they never failed to regard Ellen, who was as vivid and confident as Beth was dark and unsure of herself, as a sort of natural phenomenon, like rainbows or an eclipse. "Vincent, can you swim? Where's your tooth?" Ellen all but shouted. She kissed Jill — whom she still called 'Jilly', Chicago fashion — and shouldered half a dozen of Beth's various satchels and bags. "Let's stow everything, okay? And then Jill can take the babes for a swim or lunch or something, and we'll have a drink."

"It's one o'clock in the afternoon, Ellie!" Beth told her, embarrassed even in front of Jill.

"But we're free!" Ellen reminded her. "We're allowed to be irresponsible. We're not going to drive. We have no kids." Beth glanced at Vincent, who glowered. He did hate her. Guiltily, she reached down and pulled him against her side.

"I don't even know if I got connecting rooms," Beth told Ellen.

"You did. I stuck it all on my card."

Beth was horrified. "Ellen! You can't do that!" Ellen had money — everybody in construction was loaded, as far as Beth could tell. And though

31

it was Pat's dream to someday own part of the restaurant, and Beth's to someday run an actual photo business with real employees, they were lean now. They had been lean as long as they could remember. Once, when her brother Bick offhandedly told Beth that he and his wife had been in financial trouble, that they'd been "living paycheck to paycheck," Beth felt a stomach thump of panic. Wasn't that what everyone did? Were she and Pat supposed to have a reserve, a cushion, already? In their early thirties? Did other people?

The economic gap between Ellen and Beth usually didn't matter. Ellen sent Beth crazy things in the mail — sheets from Bloomingdale's, pounds of chocolate, five hundred dollars once, when Beth had gone crazy on the phone and cried because she couldn't buy the boys new clothes for Easter. Beth sent Ellen gallery-quality prints of her best photos; they were framed, expensively, all over Ellen's house. Ellen paid at restaurants when they ate together; she sent Kerry savings bonds as if the country were at war.

But there were times Beth balked.

"You can't pay for me," she told her friend now.

"It's, what, it's seventy bucks or something," said Ellen. "Who cares?"

"I care," Beth replied, tempted, trying to seem more genuinely proud than she actually was. "I think I can write this off, anyhow, because I have a job on Sunday. I'm shooting the antelope statues at the zoo for a brochure." Ellen's attitude reversed instantly. She was part-owner of her husband's business, after all; a write-off was a write-off.

"You're going to have to go up there in that mess and rearrange it, then," Ellen told her. They straggled into the lobby. It was jammed; virtually all the out-of-towners who'd come back for the reunion were registered there. Beth almost gave up. Dozens of people she recognized milled past her; it was like watching a movie peopled with stars from a previous era — all familiar faces, all altered, with names she couldn't summon to her tongue. Did she really want to spend fascinating moments negotiating a credit-card transaction with a twenty-two-year-old in mall bangs, who, Beth already realized, would mess the whole transaction up anyhow?

"Elizabeth — the fair Elizabeth Kerry!" The tallest man in the lobby lifted Beth off her feet. Wayne Thunder was both the first American Indian and the first homosexual Beth had ever known. "I'm gay because of you," he told her once. "Because you didn't regard me as a sex object." Wayne was a management trainer for the phone company; he was madly successful, lived in Old Town, came to spend every Thanksgiving at Beth's house.

"You have brought some children . . . " Wayne intoned. "Who are these children?" Ben and Vincent jumped up and down. They were crazy about Wayne, who brought them boxes of illegal fireworks; Beth and Pat had been asked to leave the neighborhood association after Wayne set a neighbor's hedge on fire.

Holding Ben in one arm, Wayne told Ellen and Beth conspiratorially, "I saw Cecil Lockhart. She looks just like Gloria Swanson now. She has white hair — on purpose." The antique flicker of annoyance Beth still felt at the mention of Cecil Lockhart's name took her by surprise. She realized that she had been hoping that Cecil — the swanlike, gray-eyed girl who grew up next door to Ellen, the chief and constant rival to Beth for Ellen's best friendship — would skip this occasion. Cecil (whose real name was Cecilia) was, Beth judged, the only of the Immaculata graduates from her year to have made more of herself as a creative soul than Beth had. And it rankled.

Cecil was an actress. She had taught acting at the Guthrie in Minneapolis and at the Goodman in Chicago — she was very much married. Cecil was, Ellen told Beth now, still a size six, with a belt. Ellen knew; she'd seen Cecil last year at an arts ball. Cecil had had the distinction of being the first of them ever to have sexual intercourse — at fifteen. She'd liked it. She couldn't imagine, she told Beth once, in junior year, ever going a month without doing it.

Beth noticed abruptly that the cheerleaders had arrived. They were grouped at the desk, eight of them, still a unit, as if they had moved smoothly through adult life in pyramid formation. Their husbands, all large-necked and calm, stood behind them. When they saw Beth and Ellen, they surged.

"Bethie!" called Jane Augustino, Becky Noble, Barbara Kelliher. They draped their arms around

34

Beth, whom they remembered chiefly as the short sidekick to Ellen, their Amazonian colleague, who'd inherited nothing from her Sicilian father but a name. Ellen, a revolutionary who read *Manchild in the Promised Land*, had never really embraced the soul of cheerleading; she had done it, she confided to Beth, for its surefire potential as guy bait. Even fifteen years ago, Beth couldn't have done a round-off for money. But now, she gladly embraced all the women who had formed the top tier of high-school popularity, noting carefully Barbara's chunky thighs and Becky's resolute blondness, accepting their compliments on Kerry's sunny, one-tooth smile. Then, when she spun around to grab the luggage trolley, she stumbled into Nick Palladino's chest.

"Where did you get all these kids?" he asked. Beth's stomach bubbled.

"Just made 'em with things we already had around the house," she said. She and Nick hugged; Trisha hugged her. Nick and Trisha were wearing white cotton suits that would have looked ridiculous on anyone else. On them, the suits looked like a spread in *Town and Country*.

Beth dragged Jill to her side. "Nick, this is Jill, Pat's cousin." Ellen was hugging Nick, who turned to Vincent and shook hands.

"I came this close to being your daddy," he told Vincent softly, not quite enough out of Trisha's hearing to please Beth. Beth smiled madly and concentrated on working her way to the front of the check-in line.

"My daddy is Patrick Cappadora," Vincent

told Nick with homicidal intensity.

"Jill," Beth said, "push this cart thing over by the elevator and then take the keys and park the car, okay?" She handed the baby to Ellen and lifted Vincent onto the luggage trolley. "Vincent, I want you to hold Ben's hand. Real tight. You can look around and you can stand on this funny cart. But hold his hand while Mama pays the lady. And then you can go swimming." Vincent gripped Ben's hand limply.

"I love you, Vincent," said Ben, straining to get closer to the toys in the newsstand.

Vincent smirked.

"He loves you," Beth said. "Can't you be nice?"

"I love you, Ben," said Vincent wearily. "I'm hot, Mom. My neck is killing."

And then — and Beth would never be able to banish it, no matter what other random, dangerously precious scenes she was able to sweep from her mind — Vincent had one of those flashes of egregious tenderness that he had only with Ben or Kerry, never with Beth. And never, even, with Pat, because Vincent's love for Pat didn't flicker between attachment and irritation, it was utter.

Vincent reached out and clasped Ben around his belly and pretended to get one of his fingers stuck beneath Ben's arm. "Tickle, tickle, you old fuzzhead Ben," he said, and Ben writhed in ecstasy.

Well, good, thought Beth.

She said, "This will only take one minute, now. See? Jill is getting the bags. You just stand

36

here." Nick had drifted away. She could see Ellen, a sherbet-colored crown above the other women's heads, surrounded by men, making Kerry's hand wave bye-bye, up and down. Beth pushed through the backs in front of her. The counter girl was on the phone, talking to someone at the airport, explaining nastily that no, there was no shuttle of any kind, and no, she had no idea what taxi companies operated in the area, and in any case she was very busy. Bored, she finally turned to Beth, who could barely see Vincent, bobbing up and down on the luggage trolley, and said, "Yesssss?" Beth was caught unawares; she'd been scanning the doors for a glimpse of Jill; how long did it take to park a car? She plopped her purse on the counter, nearly spilling it into the girl's lap.

It probably took five minutes. Even though the girl was slower than weight loss, even though Beth gave her a gas card by mistake first, and the girl ran it without realizing it wasn't a Visa. Absolutely not ten minutes, Beth would tell the police later, even though Beth ran into a cousin of Pat's, and her old lab partner, Jimmy Daugherty, now a cop in Parkside. Ten minutes at the outside, no more.

At last, clutching a sheaf of carbons, her wallet, and Kerry's pacifier, Beth made her way back to the elevator. Vincent was standing slumped against the wall, slowly pushing the trolley back and forth with his feet.

"Where's Ben?" she asked.

Vincent shrugged expressively. "He wouldn't let me hold him. He wanted Aunt Ellen. My neck is killing, Mom. I got a heat rash."

Absently, Beth checked his neck. It was ringed with small red blotches. "Wait," she said. She scanned the lobby for Ellen; there she was, easy to see. Beth whistled. Ellen plowed toward her, Kerry in her arms.

"Do you have Ben?" Beth asked, and she would recall later that it was not with panic. Not the way she had felt, instantly, at state fair when Ben was two and wandered away, and the crowd closed around him. She didn't feel that bottom-out sensation that preceded frenzy. Ben was in the room. The room was filled with people, all good people, grownups who knew Beth, who would ask a little kid where his mama was. "Ellen, Ben took off. We have to find him before we can do anything."

Ellen rolled her eyes and headed for the newsstand. There were toys on spinning racks there — kid bait. Beth went outside and scanned the sunny street in both directions, then came back in, circled the elevator, and darted into the deserted coffee shop. Had the lone waitress seen a little boy in a red baseball cap? No. Beth squatted down on her knees and looked through the crowd Ben-height. But all the legs ended in heels or oxfords. She ran back to the elevator, "Vincent, think hard, which way did Ben go?"

"I don't know."

"Didn't you watch?"

"I couldn't see him."

It was then that Beth's breathing came in gasps, and her hands tingled, the way they did when she'd narrowly avoided smacking another car, or almost turned her ankle. Ben! she thought. Listen to me with your mind. Ellen came slowly through the crowd, pulling Beth to her with a look.

"He wasn't over there."

"Ellenie . . . "

"We should get the manager."

"I don't know; maybe if we just wait . . . "

"No, we should get the manager."

The counter girl said the manager was at lunch, and if they wanted, they could fill out a form describing what they lost.

"What we lost is a kid!" Ellen screamed at her.

The girl said, "Whatever. The manager should be back at — "

Ellen charged across the room and leapt onto the luggage trolley. She was five feet ten, and even before she yelled "STOP!" a score of her old classmates had turned to look at her. But when she did yell, talk ceased in the lobby as if a light switch had been flicked. A phone was ringing. A bellman, outside, called, "Chuck!"

"We need to all look for Beth Kerry's little boy," Ellen said. "He's three, his name is Ben, and he was here a minute ago. He's got to be in the room. So divide up. Look all around where you are. And if you find him, pick him up and stand still."

And they all did that. They set down their bags where they were, and the whole room burst forth like a choir: "Ben? Ben?" in a shower of different timbres of voice, Beth's the loudest. Jimmy Daugherty cut the room into halves by walking through, and assigned people quadrants. Nick took off at a lope down the first-floor corridor. Twenty minutes later, a few small groups of newcomers were greeting one another again, but most of the faces nearest Beth watched her for direction, in their eyes a kind of embarrassed pity.

Ben was gone.

2

IT was Jimmy who said they might as well call the police — not that the kiddo wasn't somewhere right nearby, anyhow, but it could move things along quicker, you know? Jimmy knew everybody at Parkside; in fact, if not for the reunion, he'd be working today. "It'd be my shift, Bethie, and these are good guys. We'll get the troops over here." The station house was less than a mile away.

"Bethie, you'll feel better," he said. "He's probably asleep in a linen closet."

The manager, a chubby, fancy man, was back from lunch now. Waving his hands, with large gestures intended to play across the room, he had berated the counter slut and brought Ellen coffee — believing she was the child's mother — and checked the doors to the swimming pool to make sure they were locked, and summoned security, which turned out to be two hefty older men in ill-fitting purple livery.

Beth sat on the luggage trolley skinning her hair back from her face with her hands. In her mind's athletic eye, she was trotting the length of the corridors, shoving open every door that was ajar, calling Ben in a clear, Doris Day voice, welcoming him. In fact, her legs were gelatinous, she could not stand. Vincent was curled behind her, holding Ben's blanket, asleep. Jill had taken Kerry upstairs and put her down on a bed.

41

It was five minutes to two. Beth had been in the hotel less than one hour.

After the first, fruitless search, the lobby had drained of alums. Beth watched people slink away, talking low, not quite sure what they dared do. Were they to continue greeting each other as if nothing had happened? Join in the search? Go out to lunch? Go home? Two guys were in the bar, drinking, watching a football game on the high, slant-mounted TV; but they hadn't been here when Ben went missing. Beth didn't blame them, though she would have had she recognized them. Husbands, she thought. Not my friends.

When Jimmy came back from the desk phone, he said, "It was just what I thought. They'll send a bunch of guys over here, no problem, and they'll floor-by-floor it, and they'll find him in no time."

Ellen asked him, "What if Ben went outside?"

Jimmy looked pained. "I . . . uh . . . some guys will be looking outside, too. But Bethie, there have been no . . . accidents reported." Accidents? Beth shoved a deck of her brain over to accommodate new alarm. He could have been run down by a car, picked up by a felon, knocked into a ditch, flattened by a train . . . Beth seized herself, forcibly. She tended to embrace panic as a matter of course; Kerrys did that — no hangnail was too small for a short fulmination.

But Ben had been missing now for one full hour. Ben had never, unless Beth was on a job or out for dinner twice a year with Pat or giving birth, been out of Beth's sight for one full hour, in the three years of his life.

So this was serious. Too serious for panic. Beth needed to call upon the self that, in her newspaper days, calmly started printing photos of a fire at midnight and finished by one a.m., in time for the first press run. The self that once found a way to pull and snap Vincent's dislocated arm back into place, while his limb dangled like a plunger on a rubber band. Who stanched bleeding foreheads, who made children who ate muscle relaxants throw them up. That self struggled in her grasp and broke free. She smoothed her face. It welled with oil, as if she hadn't washed for days.

The clock, meanwhile, lurched ahead. In the moment that she spent on her face, another eight minutes passed.

Ben had been missing for one hour and eight minutes.

"Bethie," Jimmy was saying, deliberately casual. "This is Calvin Taylor. He's my partner. Everybody's coming. Slow day at the old station house. Cal, this is Beth Cappadora. It's her boy."

Beth looked up; she felt small, like a pond resident. It felt good to look up, good to be down where she could do nothing, ruin nothing, take charge of nothing. She wondered if Taylor could see her at all. Calvin Taylor was slender and spectacled, spoke with a Jamaican lilt. "Don't worry, mother," he said genially. "We haven't lost a child yet."

He squatted down next to Beth and asked

her a series of soft questions about Ben — his size, his age, his clothing, where he was standing when she last saw him. Beth murmured in reply. When Wayne came over, Calvin Taylor shook his hand and asked about the results of the first-floor search. And then he said, again genially, "Well, Mr. Thunder, sounds like nothing left for us to do but open a few doors." Wayne all but beamed with pride; the police had commended him! Beth almost laughed aloud.

Jimmy and Taylor told the manager, who was lurking, to get a passkey; they would have to open two hundred rooms.

"Ah, there are guests, though . . . " the manager said nervously.

"We'll knock," said Taylor.

The lobby filled with handsome young men — almost all short, Irish, Italian, a couple of black guys, one tall Germanic blond. A woman with long brown hair in a bun, looking awkward in a uniform clearly not styled to fit the contours of her body. She came over and sat down beside Beth on the trolley. "Scared, huh?" she said. "Don't worry. We'll find him. I mean, I've been a cop for five years, and I've looked for a dozen kids, and we always find them." She stopped and looked at Beth, who was pulling her own hair now, rhythmically. "We find them, and they're okay. Not hurt."

Beth did not know what to do with Vincent; she supposed she should comfort him. She looked at him, as he twitched in his sleep.

"Would you like something to eat?" the manager asked Ellen. He was florid now, and smelled thickly of cigarette smoke.

"I'm not his mother," Ellen told him. The manager, now sighing audibly, turned to Beth.

"Would you like something to eat?"

Beth considered. She did not see how it would be possible to eat.

"I'd like a vodka and tonic," she said. The manager's mouth made an O in surprise, but he bustled off, literally snapping his fingers to the bartender.

"Paperwork," said the brown-haired police officer with the artful bun. "I have to ask you a couple of things, Mrs. Cappadora. I mean, even if we find him in five minutes, there has to be a report, of course. And we need the most detailed description we can get to send out to other departments — if we need to do that, which we probably won't."

Beth knew she was supposed to find this soothing, this routine-ness, this scoffing at the absurdity of it all. It was meant to assure her that any minute a tousled Ben, with a fistful of baseball cards given him by a friendly policeman, would be carried out the elevator doors like a silver cup. Everyone would be smiling, everyone would be chiding Ben, 'You gave your mama a scare, partner . . .'

" . . . three?" asked the police officer.

"Yes," said Beth. "What?"

"He's three, your son?"

"Just turned."

"Date of birth?"

"April first."

"April Fool's Day."

45

"Yep."

"And he has, what . . . brown hair?"

"He has red hair. He has dark red hair. Auburn. And a red baseball cap. He's wearing an orange shirt with red fish on it. And purple shorts. And red high-top gym shoes. Those are new. Parrots." Beth bit her lip; she knew how that sounded — as though she didn't care enough to match colors in her kids' outfits. But who noticed what a kid wore to ride in a car? She slid her eyes over to the brown-haired officer. *She* would. The officer was probably a caring mother.

And why, she asked herself suddenly, don't they tell one another what Ben looks like? Is there a therapy or a strategy in the repetition?

"And Mrs. Cappadora, where did you say you lived?"

Beth hunkered down and talked. She concentrated on precision and detail. She pretended she was Pat. She told the officer about Ben's language skills and his fears (windstorms, all bodies of water, blood) and his habit of hiding in small places (once, horrifyingly, but just for a moment, the dryer). In detail, she described Ben's birthmark, the mark in the shape of a nearly perfect carat — an ashy-colored inverted V that sat just above his left hip. The birthmark had been something Beth considered having removed, she told the officer, but the dermatologist said it was nothing, just an excess of pigment, and so she left it alone. Sensing the officer's restlessness, Beth next talked about Vincent — who had awakened

46

and gone off with Ellen to get a sandwich. He was a difficult kid, but he loved Ben and was protective of him.

"Kerry's named after me," said Beth. "I mean, not Beth, but that's my last name, Kerry. Before I got married. We were going to name Ben that, Kerry . . . at least I wanted to, but Pat — that's my husband — he said, 'Why not just name him Fairy?' So we named the girl that instead. Ben's named after my brother . . . " She babbled; the lobby was filling up again, with police officers Beth hadn't seen before.

As Beth watched, two of them set up a folding table in a small room off the lobby that probably was used to hold coats with a number of cellular phones and a compact radio that squawked and crackled.

"What are they doing?" Beth asked.

"They're setting up a command center," a young female officer whose name tag read G. Clemons, told her.

"What for?"

"Well, to stay in touch with the station, and to take any calls that might come in from the state police or other departments."

"Other departments?"

"Yes. Or tips from people. Or any kind of calls. I mean, if we knew for sure that anybody else had been involved in this, it'd probably be a larger operation already. But the kind of tips we're going to be getting might — "

"Tips? But how would anyone know where to call?" Beth asked, and then what G. Clemons had alluded to jabbed her. One person might.

47

"Just a minute, Mrs. Cappadora." Tucking stray ends into the careful roll at the back of her head, Officer Clemons spoke briefly with Detective Taylor. He took the sheet of paper she'd been using, made a few jottings on it himself, and took off for the phone.

"We're putting out an ISPEN, Mrs. Cappadora. That's 'Illinois State Police Emergency Network'. Alphabet soup, huh?" The bun bobbed in concern. Beth thought, she's still trying not to scare me. "That frequency is monitored by all departments statewide. For example, this is District Three, near Chicago, but we pick up way into the western and northern suburbs . . ."

"You have a lot of police officers for such a little city."

"Oh, these aren't all Parkside police, Mrs. Cappadora," said Officer Clemons. "They're from Chester and Barkley and Rosewell, too."

Beth stared at her. "So you're worried."

"We have to take the disappearance of a child this small, after this length of time, very, very seriously, Mrs. Cappadora."

It was three p.m. Ben had been missing for two hours.

There were two cops at each of the exits Beth could see, and the slice of the circle drive that lay inside her vision was filling with blue-and-white cars, like a puzzle with pieces sliding into place. Jimmy Daugherty crossed in front of the revolving door. Beth excused herself and wobbled, thickly, to his side. She asked Jimmy for a Marlboro. He lit it.

48

"Bethie," he said. "Pat will be here soon, right?"

Beth was startled. "I didn't call him."

Jimmy ground out his own cigarette with a vicious twist of thumb and forefinger. "You didn't call Pat?"

"I thought we'd find him right away, and Pat had to work." She sounded like the kind of light-witted ninny who would soon begin to complain that she was missing her favorite soap. She tried again: "No one told me to call Pat!" That was worse. In the valley of the gathering shadow, who doesn't call your nearest? The child's father?

"Let's call now," Jimmy told her gently.

Beth thought, well, I'm not going to.

"And your folks? They're all still here, huh?"

Not them, either, thought Beth. No chance.

Pat would not have left a three-year-old to wander off alone. He would have made quick, fail-safe preparations — waved Ellen over, or waited to leave Vincent and Ben with Jill. He would have given the three minutes that safety demanded, not waded off blunderingly the way Beth did, trying to cut corners, shave time, consolidate motions. He would not do what Beth did when she set a hot glass dish on a corner of the counter at home and tried to make one phone call and then let the dish fall. He was full of foresight.

All their parents knew that.

Beth said no, she would not bother their parents now.

"I guess that's probably best, actually," said

49

Jimmy. "Because you could have a family situation here, where the grandparents wanted the child — I mean, Bethie, I'm probably not exercising the kind of judgment I usually do because I know you and Pat and the Cappadoras. But who knows? Actually, my supervisor said the first thing I talked to her that we have to get somebody over to their house and talk to them."

"To Rosie and Angelo Cappadora's?"

"Right. Pat's folks. I know them, but we don't need to broadcast that we're coming."

"You mean you think that Rosie and Angelo could have Ben?"

"Anything's possible. A family feud — "

"Oh, that's so nuts, Jimmy. Rosie and Angelo worship Ben."

"That's just what I mean."

"And there's nothing with Pat and me or anything. They don't even know I'm in Chicago. Neither does my dad."

"People do strange things, Bethie."

Cop wisdom. Full-moon talk. This was all happening too quickly. All these people were too concerned all of a sudden. Couldn't Jimmy see how time-wasting and absurd it would be to send a police car to Rosie and Angelo's manicured ranch house to ask them if they'd stolen their grandson whom they didn't even know was in town? Didn't Jimmy grasp that she didn't want to see her dad or Pat's parents? To have them see her? She had always seemed unusual to Angelo, unusual to her father, perhaps even to Rosie, who liked everyone. But now, with this, if the

50

parents came, there would be no escaping.

Jimmy led her to the telephone, wrote down Beth's home number in Madison, and dialed it for her. But when the phone began to burr, she felt as if she would have diarrhea, right there, and handed the receiver to Jimmy. Ellen came back and took her to the bathroom, and because Beth's legs would not bend, actually helped her sit down. Then Beth went into the bar and ordered another vodka and tonic; she didn't even attempt to pay. She had no idea where her purse was, or her shoes. Or Jill. Nick Palladino had come down and brought Vincent a small football on a rubberized string. Vincent was batting it up and down. Wayne and Nick and a couple of the cheerleaders' husbands stood around the bar. Beth watched their jaws work up and down.

" . . . to help," said Nick.

"Huh?" asked Beth.

"She's torn up. She wants to go home," said Nick. "But I'll come back."

Trisha wants to go home to the children, Beth thought. To their two little girls, make sure they are safe, hold them and smell them. She said, "No, you don't have to. Unless you want to go to the party."

"Oh, Beth, I don't think they'll have the party," said Nick. "At least, not unless they find Ben, you know?"

So grave. So grave so fast. Grave enough, this perhaps-not-temporary loss of her child, to cancel a year-planned event for two hundred couples? If it's so grave as that, Beth thought,

51

logically I should cry. She tried to let her eyes fill. But they would only lock, pasted open, staring at Nick's suit buttons, which had little, silver whales on them.

"I'd do anything for you, Beth," Nick told her.

"Oh, okay," Beth answered. Was that an appropriate reply? She searched Nick's face. His beautiful eyes looked puzzled. I should have married Nick, Beth thought, no matter how unintellectual he is. Then I wouldn't have had Ben to lose. That would be better. Her glass was empty.

Jimmy Daugherty came back and said he'd phoned Pat — Pat wasn't home.

"You have to call the restaurant."

"You guys have a restaurant?"

"His uncle's. Cappadora's. 741-3333."

Jimmy wrote it down. On the way to the phone, he added, "Don't worry, Bethie. Look around you. The Marines are here! And bliss is coming."

He sounded sure. She sipped her drink, prudently.

Ellen had ordered a pizza. Vincent wanted pizza, and the hotel didn't serve it. Discipio's was only a mile or so away, said Ellen. Jill, she told Beth, was lying down . . . upset. Ellen had given Kerry to Barbara Kelliher. "And don't worry, Beth, she's right in her room, number 221, and Becky's with her. Kerry's safe, Beth."

Beth decided against telling Ellen that it didn't matter; she didn't really care whether Kerry was safe, unless Ben was found. She said, "Oh, good."

Wayne, the police, and the purple security men were rounding up everyone in the hotel who was connected with the reunion; they'd assemble in the ballroom, for what Beth pictured as a sort of ghastly dress rehearsal of the evening's planned assembly. The police would make small groups and then search the hotel rooms left vacant once again, in case they'd missed something. Everyone not connected with the reunion had been shuttled to the Parkside Arms, three blocks away, because the ordinary customers, only half a dozen couples, had been unnerved by the droves of uniforms in the lobby and the cordons outside.

The manager was furious and kept asking when the investigation would be complete. "Hasn't started yet, buddy," Jimmy told him.

"I thought this place didn't have a shuttle," Beth remarked to Ellen.

Ellen stared at her, glared at her. "What?"

"Never mind." Beth's glass was empty. She held it up and Ellen took it to the bar.

It was five p.m. Ben had been missing four hours.

Beth could feel her stomach boiling; she was actively nauseated; she probably needed to stop drinking. But there was the process of getting smaller, which had started when she first met the sergeant. That was wise to continue, Beth knew for sure. She accepted another drink from Nick. The brown-haired bun officer was back.

"Now, Mrs. Cappadora . . . " she began.

53

"Beth," said Beth. It was such a long name, hers and Pat's; if she kept using it, this would take all night. Night. No, not yet. Outside the window, it was still bright afternoon, the sun spilling wavelike over the round shadow caves made by the hotel awnings.

"Well, you can call me Grace then," said the bun.

"Grace Clemons," said Beth.

"Right!" said the officer, as if Beth were very, very bright for her age. "One thing that sometimes happens is, parents sometimes have fingerprints taken of their children — "

"Fingerprints?" Beth shouted. The lobby went still for a long instant; then a phone rang and the burble of voices quietly resumed. And then Beth remembered: "I did, actually. We had this school program — Identa-Kid, through Dane County. We did both boys."

Beth thought Grace Clemons might literally jump up and down. "That's so wonderful, Mrs. Cappadora! Now we have a good tool, a real helper, for finding Ben."

Am I thick, Beth thought, or is she talking to me in layers? If they were to find Ben, why, they would bring Ben to his mother, and he would wrap his legs around me like a cub on a trunk. Who would need fingerprints? Fingerprints were for criminals — and victims.

Beth felt as if she heard a far-off engine sputter and then catch. That was it. So far, so fast. Children taken to hospitals, found in weeds, children whose hands were not damaged, but their faces . . .

54

"Now, this Identa-Kid program, Mrs. Cappadora, would that be through your local police department?"

"Uh, no — Dane County, I said."

"County sheriff?"

"Yes."

"And that's which county?"

"*Dane* County." Didn't I just say this? Beth wondered.

Grace Clemons summoned one of the cops manning the phones and told him to get in touch with Dane County stat and get a fingerprint fax. You don't understand, Beth wanted to explain. I had Ben's fingerprints taken so that he would not ever be stolen or lost. It was preventive medicine, kept in the cabinet like Ipecac, to ward off poison by the fact of its presence; it was not ever intended to be used.

The brown-haired bun was talking again. Clemons. Yes. Grace. "Tell me what happened when you first came into the hotel, Now, your friend Elaine — "

"Ellen."

"Ellen was with you?"

"She met me in the parking lot."

"In the parking lot?" said Grace Clemons. "How did she know you were in the parking lot?"

"Well, she was looking for me. She would come out and look, and go back in. And then we got here."

"And besides Ellen, who was the first person you talked to?"

"Well, my boyfriend . . . I mean, my ex . . . I

mean, my boyfriend from high school, Nick. And Wayne. My friend Wayne. He's Pat's friend, too. And the cheerleaders." Grace Clemons looked disappointed. Beth wondered what she'd done wrong. Her glass was empty. She held it up. Ellen materialized from somewhere and took it.

Beth said, "I have to get up for a minute."

Jimmy Daugherty had somehow found time to take off his suit and put on an ordinary summer-weight jacket and shirt. Jimmy was still as lean as the swimmer he'd been senior year, with crisp brown curls and a Marine-recruitment-poster jaw. Beth thought absurdly of Superman, ducking into the cloak room. He had told Beth he was a detective in plainclothes, and these were certainly plain. He'd even showed her his gold shield, as if to reassure her that they were both grownups now and not going to fight about who had to pith the frog in lab.

Now Jimmy approached Beth with a tall, willowy woman, ash-blond, with the kind of languid, manicured hands Beth associated with the Shorewood mothers for whom she sometimes shot photos of garden festivals. She wore a short plaid skirt and a long cotton sweater. He's going to introduce me to his wife, thought Beth. Is this possible? And then she remembered, Jimmy was married to the little Ricarelli girl, Anita — a child bride who had given him four boys before her thirtieth birthday.

"Beth, this is my boss," Jimmy told her. "This is Detective Supervisor Bliss."

"I'm not really his boss — who could boss

Jimmy? I just head up the detectives," said the woman, smiling.

"You're a police chief?" she asked stupidly.

"No, just of detectives . . . Well, my name is Candy Bliss."

Beth laughed, snorted; she couldn't help it, but was instantly mortified.

The woman's green eyes lighted with a kind of conspiratorial joy. "I know — it sounds like a stripper, huh? My sister's name is Belle, can you beat that? Belle Bliss? I'm the stripper; she's the gun moll. The stuff parents can do to you, huh?"

She stopped, and pressed one slender finger against a deep line just between her arched brows. "I can't believe I said that. Mrs. Cappadora, I want you to know, we are going to find your little boy. Can we sit down?" Jimmy drifted away.

"Jimmy doesn't have to work; he took a night off," Beth said helplessly. She did not want Candy Bliss to think her a greedy person.

"Oh, I think he wants to," said Candy Bliss. She gave Beth her dazzling smile, then turned to Grace Clemons, and Beth saw the smile vanish, as if Bliss had run a washcloth over her face.

She said, "Description?"

Grace Clemons said, "Already out, and they're doing the leads now."

"What leads?" Beth asked. "Who saw him?"

"Not those kinds of leads, Mrs. Cappadora. It's a computer network," Candy Bliss explained. "Law Enforcement Agency Data Systems. If anyone were to be able to run this child by obtaining his name or date of birth — "

"He has no idea what his date of birth is."

"Well, his name, then — it would come back on the computer as a hit. We'd have a location for him."

"A location?"

"A hospital, if he got hurt — a lone child if he was picked up by a unit." She turned her attention back to the other woman. "Detective Clemons, I can take over here now. I'm going to want you to do press if this keeps up for very much longer, so start preparing a statement." She shot a look at Beth. "Ben answers to his name?"

"Yes."

"So I guess, maybe, okay, use the name, and heavy on the description. Just . . . let me have a look at it before you go with it."

Switch. Turn. Radiant smile again. "Now," she said, "here's the deal."

Odds strongly favored finding Ben within the next hour or so. "Children disappear all the time. Even in a little town like this. We have kids wander off from the carnival, from the playground, the library. From day care — there's major hell to pay when that happens. They walk down the block, turn the wrong way, and get lost. The thing is, someone always finds them. And what we're seeing now, I think, is just that gap in time between someone finding Ben and bringing him to a police station, or calling the police while they have Ben at their house . . . "

"So you're saying you think he's no longer in

the hotel, period," Beth began.

"It's been a little too long for that now. And this search has been pretty thorough."

The next step, said Candy Bliss, would be to create target maps of the immediately surrounding area; then search systematically — go door to door along the short block of stores that ran parallel to the cemetery, cut over to the high school to check the sports equipment sheds, the fields, the bleachers, any place that might attract a kid's attention.

"There are a lot of fathers and grandfathers here who are pretty upset," said the detective. "We're getting a fair number of volunteers dropping in who are off-shift tonight. By the way, that's why it took me so long to get here. I wasn't working tonight. I apologize. It was my nephew's birthday, way up in Algonquin."

"Oh, I'm sorry." Beth nodded.

"You mean, to take me away from it? Oh come on, that's fine. He got what he wanted out of me anyway. Little Tykes wagon."

"Ben has that, too. Santa Claus. How old is your little nephew?"

"Well, actually, he's three today. He's three."

Beth reached for her glass and drained her drink.

The pizza arrived then.

It was five-thirty, Ben had been missing four hours and thirty minutes.

The pizza delivery kid in his red-and-yellow smock barely made it through the revolving glass door when Pat flew in as if out of a hailstorm and jostled the kid to one knee. It was 150 miles

59

from the restaurant to Parkside, maybe more. Pat would later tell Beth he didn't really know how fast he drove; but she calculated it had to be close to a hundred miles an hour. No one stopped him; he paid no tolls. He left the door of the freezer open at Cappadora's and the lip of the cash register hanging out, the tray stuffed with money. Augie wasn't there, only a seventeen-year-old waitress and the busboy, Rico.

"Where is he?" asked Pat of the manager, who happened to be the first person in his line of vision.

"The little boy?" said the manager. "You'll have to talk to the police about that matter."

"Paddy," said Jimmy Daugherty with the kind of easy, instant intimacy Beth craved from fellow Irish. "We haven't found him yet. It shouldn't take long, though."

"What?" Pat cried. "What? Where's Ben? Where's Beth?"

Hastily, Beth stuck her half-filled glass behind her and scrambled to her feet. Pat rushed at her, grabbed her, held the back of her skull in his free hand as if she were a child. "Bethie," he told her, speaking slowly, as if she were hearing-impaired, "tell me how this happened. Tell me where Ben is."

Beth made a small motion; should she shrug, try to speak? Explain?

Pat let her go, not entirely gently, and said, "Okay. Okay. Can I smoke in here?" Four people offered him a light. "Okay, okay," Pat said again. "Now, where is there in the hotel

60

nobody has searched? The basement?"

"Just food storage down there," said the manager. "And it's locked. All the doors leading to storage are locked from the outside."

"Ben would love food storage. He grew up in a restaurant. Freezers and cabinets." He gestured to the manager. "You take me there."

"I don't see why," said the manager.

"We were going to anyway," said Calvin Taylor, appearing. As they walked off, Vincent appeared screaming, "Daddy!"

Pat waved for Vincent to stay back, stay with his mother.

"Your husband," said Candy Bliss. "That's okay. He needs to do something. We all do. And what we'll do is just go through that first half-hour once more. Is that okay, Beth?"

This was liturgy, then. Christ have mercy upon us. Lord have mercy upon us. Mercy upon us as many ways and by as many names as possible, over and over. Beth's part was to answer.

Had she seen Ben wander off? Had Vincent? Did Ben have a history of attention deficit or other neurological disorders? Did Ben have seizures? Was he drawn to shiny objects?

Seizures? Shiny objects?

"Huh?" Beth asked her. "Of course he liked shiny objects. All kids like shiny objects." She explained to Candy Bliss that she had seen nothing, nothing but one glimpse from the check-in desk of Vincent's head bobbing up and down.

"Well, then let's ask Mister Vincent," said

61

Candy Bliss. She got up and settled herself on the luggage trolley, where Vincent cringed. "You wanta help the cops, Vincent? We got a lost brother here." Vincent stared around her, at Beth. Beth nodded faintly. "First, I want you to point for me in which direction Ben walked away."

Vincent sat back down on the luggage trolley and coiled back against the wall beside the elevator, hiding his eyes with uncharacteristic reluctance, until Beth walked over and settled him on her lap. Then he buried his face against Beth's midriff and violently shook his head. Beth eased him up and brushed the sweaty hair off his forehead.

"You can help find Ben. Old fuzzhead Ben needs you," she told him. Vincent squeezed his eyes closed; like her, Beth thought, he wanted to shrink to a dot.

"He's shrinking," she told Candy Bliss, who blinked once, quickly, and then looked away.

"Come on, buddy," the detective urged Vincent. "Show me where your brother went."

Vincent stuck out one limp and skinny arm and pointed toward the center of the room.

If Ben had toddled — Beth caught herself using the word, making Ben tinier, more babylike than he really was — off in that direction, he would have come gradually closer and closer to Beth.

He had been trying to come to Beth.

"Did you poke him?" Beth asked Vincent, suddenly, ferociously.

"No, I didn't touch him one single time!"

62

"Was he frightened? Did he want me?"

"No — Ellen. He wanted me to get Aunt Ellen. He said he was peeing his pants."

Beth loosed her arms from around Vincent; he flopped forward. She clawed her face again — Ben helpless, Ben embarrassed and looking for a trusted grownup, any of his 'safe grownups', to help him use the bathroom. Had he seen her? Had he called? Had he tried to find a washroom on his own? Beth stood up, reeled, sat down heavily on the luggage trolley.

"I can think of better places to fall than that thing," Bliss said. "Why don't we get you on a couch?"

Lie down, Beth thought. It was the suggestion you made all the time in disasters, to people waiting to hear about the survivors of downed aircraft, to the stranded, to those in hospital emergency rooms awaiting the results of doomed surgeries. Have coffee. Lie down. Try to eat something. She had said it herself, to Pat's cousin (Jill's mother, Rachelle) last year, when Jill, then a freshman, had been hit by a car on her bike and had a leg broken in three places. Rachelle had listened; she lay down and slept.

Beth supposed she should lie down; her throat kept filling with nastiness and her stomach roiled. But if she lay down, she wanted to explain to Candy Bliss, who was holding out her hand, it would be deserting Ben. Did Detective Bliss think Ben was lying down? If Beth ate, would he eat? She should not do anything Ben couldn't do or was being prevented from doing. Was he crying? Or wedged in a dangerous and

63

airless place? If she lay down, if she rested, wouldn't Ben feel her relaxing, think she had decided to suspend her scramble toward him, the concentrated thrust of everything in her that she held out to him like a life preserver? Would he relax then, turn in sorrow toward a bad fate, because his mama had let him down?

Surely this woman would understand how urgently Beth needed to remain upright.

She smiled brightly at Candy Bliss and said, "He's not dead."

"No, of course not, Beth."

"If he were dead, I could tell. A mother can tell."

"That's what they say."

"It's true, though. They talk to you with their minds, your kids. You wake up before they wake up — not because you hear them cry; you hear them getting ready to cry." Beth had never thought about the sinister extension of that link before — that if Ben were now being tortured or suffocating, she would feel a searing pain in her, perhaps in her belly, her throat. She was, instantly, entirely sure of this; there would be a physical alert, a signal at the cellular level. She strained up on the end of her spine, to raise her aerial, her sensors. She felt nothing, smelled and heard nothing, not even a whisper of breathed air past her ear.

And then Pat came up out of the basement of the hotel, yelling, "Where's your phone? I have to call my father and mother, and my cousin, my sisters!"

No, Beth thought, not them all. And yet,

perhaps, if they came — and then went — she could follow her feelers, delicate feelers deranged by all this light and sound, into the night, clear. She could rise up from this pond bottom, from where she watched Pat, and let Ben pull her to him. Pull his mother to him with the gravitational force of their bond.

It was seven p.m.

She watched as Vincent soundlessly, furiously threw himself on Pat — and Pat had sufficient presence of will to show love for Vincent even now, to bury his face in Vincent's neck. "Don't worry, Vincenzo," he said. "Papa will find Ben."

Mama, Beth thought. Mama will find Ben. Maybe.

She leaned forward, delicately and slowly, over the edge of the luggage trolley, and vomited on the tile floor in front of the elevator.

3

ITALIANS were good at this sort of thing. In a jam, Irish would tremble and supplicate theatrically; but Italians knew what mattered in this world: that everyone needed food and shelter, that an army ran on its stomach, that children had to be bathed and put to bed. Except at funerals, when they indulged hysteria at a time when it availed them least, Italians did what needed doing.

Beth's mother-in-law, Rosie, came in the revolving door carrying the car keys. She'd driven. Angelo would have wanted to, but he was older than she by ten years, a little loose behind the wheel at the best of times. Rosie, who was boss, didn't trust him in a crisis.

Rosie was little, light-boned, not at all the stereotypic black-shawled Sicilian mama — she had a pageboy, and wore a silver-moon pin on her plum-colored jacket. She looked chic, thought Beth, and collected, as she patted Beth's cheek and murmured *"Carissima"* and exchanged a look with Pat (no words necessary). Then, without asking for a progress report — Rosie assumed she would get that if there were progress — she took the elevator upstairs to fetch Jill and Kerry. Jill's mother, Rachelle, Rosie's niece, was at the house. Jill would be happier with her mother. Ellen offered to ask her husband, Dan, to come for Vincent, so he could play with her son, David; but Rosie silenced her with a smile. "Vincenzo will go to the house, Ellenie dear," she said. "It's better."

Ellen, who had known Rosie all her life, would not have thought of arguing.

For Beth, there was an almost festive interval when Rosie arrived. She knew she smelled of puke and booze; but Rosie, who normally frosted her eyes to behavior she called 'stupida,' had not noticed, or had chosen to overlook. Angelo barreled in with a tray of cream horns for the police and set them down on the table where the phone bank burred steadily. The officers smiled faintly, exchanging looks. Beth thought, They don't understand: you give something, you get something. They'll remember the cream horns and make one more call.

Angelo grabbed Beth and searched her face, kissed Pat on the mouth. "My God in heaven," he said. He ripped the paper covering from the cream horns. One was out of place; Angelo, by long habit, turned it and set it in line with the others.

Rosie and Angelo were first-generation, but far more pragmatic than earthy. They were caterers; it was not possible for a Mob wedding to take place on the west side without Rosie and Angelo's braciole and cream horns, their ice swans (tinted) and Champagne fountain. And not just Mob — Rosie and Angelo did weddings for ordinary Catholics who weren't even Italian, and for Protestants and Jews. They marinated chicken breasts in mustard and red vinegar; they sprinkled nasturtiums in the salad bowls before anyone else did it; they made a miniature of the towering wedding cake for the bride and groom to freeze and to thaw at the birth of the first child. They knew how to do things.

They had never had a child mortally ill or a grandchild lost. They had been married forty years, and for all Beth knew, their life's severest tragedy had been the death of her own mother, their dearest friend. Even so, Beth could see they would do the right thing. They would help find Ben and they would forgive her.

By contrast, Beth's father, Bill, was red-faced and dazed when he arrived. Not because of the crisis; he'd been golfing, with the firefighters — he'd been a chief, through most of Beth's childhood, though he was retired now ten years. Beth had not even told Bill she'd be in town — she had the job to shoot, after all, and the reunion dinner and brunch would consume all the time up to that. "What are you doing, sweetheart?" he asked Beth, straightening his sweater and leaning down to take Beth's hands. "What is this about Ben? Is he in the hospital?"

Rosie had left a message at the nineteenth hole, and a kid had run out in a cart to bring Bill in.

"Bill, Ben's missing . . . " Pat told him.

"Missing? But Ben's only two. Where?"

"He's three, Bill. Here. They think he's somewhere in the hotel . . . "

"Is he three? That's right. Did somebody call the police?"

Pat sighed.

"Well, sure," Bill went on. "I see all the blues. Did somebody call Stanley?" Stanley was the chief of police in Chester, the west-side suburb where Bill had served as fire chief for twenty-three years.

"It's Parkside, Bill," Pat told him. "They got this jurisdiction. But there's Chester police here, and Barkley, too. Even Rosewell."

"Well, but Stanley could help out." Bill could never be anything less than pugnaciously certain that a guy he knew could put matters straight. These cops, they looked young, he told Pat.

"Where were you, Patrick, when the baby walked away? Where was Beth?"

Ellen explained the whole thing to him then, while Beth got up and wandered into the bar. She could see the bartender scan her denim shirt, which was still damp and stained where Ellen had sponged away the vomit. But the bartender, a Hispanic guy with an elaborate mustache, gave her the vodka and tonic she asked for.

"Rosie!" Bill bawled when Rosie came back down into the hall, carrying the sleeping Kerry, leading Jill, who was holding Vincent's hand and carrying his football and overnight bag. "What's going on, sweetie? What's all this?"

"Give Grandpa a kiss, Vincenzo," Rosie told Vincent, and Vincent, who was ordinarily shy at first around Bill, turned up his face to be kissed. Bill picked Vincent up and embraced Angelo.

"Ange, what's this? Where's the baby?"

Beth slammed the drink. She didn't feel a

flicker of tipsiness, or even nausea — the liquor descended tenderly, like hot chocolate. She began to grow small again. Her father was not rising to the moment; it was his habit to act as if the world perplexed him. Beth was sure it did not; it was only Bill's way of getting someone else to manage. When her mother was dying, Bill stood in the hospital hall, his face collapsed in a frown, while doctors explained that Mrs. Kerry needed dialysis, and even that, perhaps, would not clear the —

"Wait," Bill had told them. "This cyst, if you remove this cyst, why then . . . ?"

There was an almost comic quality to the combination of unlucky breaks and Bill's bewilderment at each of them. Did we say two weeks? she imagined the doctors telling her father. We meant two days. Every palliative surgery, every new regimen of antibiotics intended to drive off the deepening infection revealed another complication, another mass of necrotic tissue, another absence of function. The doctors continued to probe and prop and confer. Bill continued to ask them when Evie would be cured, not how much time was left. Beth and her brothers, Paul and Bick, floundered, pitying Bill for his vacuity, hating him for it, wanting him to take charge of them as he did a squad at an industrial fire, wanting to take charge themselves and shake him, tell him, "Dad, she's dying."

But the train of Evelyn's illness kept careening downhill; and still, Bill was perplexed when Evelyn died. "She doesn't look like she could be filled with poison," he told Beth at the funeral

70

parlor. "Does she? Does this figure?"

He looked at Beth this same way now. As if she would clear matters up for him.

"We got an unidentified. Elmwood Hospital," one of the stocky younger officers called. Everyone stopped. Candy Bliss was across the lobby like a sprinter, taking the phone. "Yes, a boy . . . No, I don't think so." She scanned the room for Beth. "Can Ben speak Spanish?" Beth shook her head and the detective asked her, an instant later, as if inspired by a random thought, "How about Italian?"

"Just swear words," said Pat. No one laughed. Pat said then, "He speaks English. *Sesame Street* English."

"We'll call you back," Candy Bliss said.

The child was older, she told Beth. He'd been hit by a car riding a bike; he was in stable condition. Had to be four or five at least. And Elmwood was ten miles away, easy. But he did have auburn hair. Beth looked up at her. Candy Bliss pressed a forefinger between her eyes. "Jimmy!" she called. "You saw Ben, right? Take a run over there and look at this little boy, okay? What's the harm?"

Jimmy was already grabbing for his coat.

"Who are all those people calling?" Beth asked.

"Mostly other departments, calling back to tell us what they've been hearing, that's all," said Candy Bliss. "Later, when . . . well, if we have to inform the press, we'll get a whole ton of calls from everyone, including Elvis, saying he's seen Ben."

71

"Cranks."

"Aliens. The Easter bunny. And genuinely lonely people who watch reality TV shows."

"And what if one of them has?"

"That's why we listen to the Easter bunny."

Past them proceeded an almost mournful parade of half-familiar faces, refugees from the reunion. A few people were staying, Ellen had told her, mostly those who were going to stay over a few days anyhow. And they wanted to help. But the majority of the people were going home, or out in large groups for dinner.

"Can we still stay here?" Beth asked. She wanted to be good, the model complainant, the kind of patient the dentist liked best because she kept her mouth open so wide.

"Of course, absolutely." She smiled at Pat. Now he had to hear the recounting, find out about the odds. "Anyhow, it's a beautiful night out there; he wouldn't even really be uncomfortable."

Beth gaped at the clock.

It was 9:15. Ben had been missing for eight hours. A work day. A day of school. An amount of time that would not be accidental. She jumped up, sweating. "It's so late!"

"That's what I mean, Mrs. Cappadora. In a sense, that's an advantage. Now it's quiet out there, and we can really start getting a sense of what's going on in the town. The canine unit is on the way, and we're getting helicopter support from Chicago. We have a neighborhood patrol, too — "

"Helicopters?" Beth asked.

72

"Equipped with infrared sensors, Beth. When things quiet down, they can scan open areas. They pick up objects that are giving off heat. A person, lying down maybe."

"Or a person dead."

"Or a body, yes. But that's not what we're looking for here. We want to be able to pick up a sign of Ben even if he is trying to hide from being seen, for example, in some bushes. See?" She excused herself for a moment and whispered to one of the cops on the phone, almost too low for Beth to hear, "Are they *breeding* the goddamn dogs or what?"

"Where's Rosie?" Beth asked Pat, gripping his hand, which was icy and wet. "Where's Rosie?"

Rosie was about to leave, to take the children home. But she came to Beth, humming so softly it sounded like a purr, and pushed Beth's tangled hair behind her ears as if Beth were a little girl. In Jill's arms, Kerry was absorbed in her bottle, but Rosie took Vincent firmly by the hand and told him, "Kiss Mama. You'll see Mama soon. We'll go to sleep at Nana's."

His eyes were wired with overtiredness, and something else, a confusion she had never seen before in her linear-minded eldest. Vincent leaned over. Beth hugged him perfunctorily; but for an instant, surprising her, he clung. Then Vincent took Rosie's hand and walked a few steps without looking back. All at once he stopped.

"Mom?" he called.

73

Beth heard him, but had no energy for an answer.

"Mom?" Vincent called again, conversationally. "Did Ben get back yet?"

Rosie said firmly, "Not quite yet. Very soon." But Vincent was looking straight at Beth's eyes, his comically too-bushy brows drawn down in absorbed attention.

"Mom," he said, "I asked you a thing. Did Ben get back yet?"

Beth said, "Sweetheart. No."

Vincent said, "Oh."

Beth covered her face, scoured it with her fingers. She looked down at her nails. The creamy-coral guaranteed-two-week manicure was smudged and split.

Angelo and Bill didn't leave. They stayed in the lobby, sprawled in armchairs, though the manager officiously encouraged everyone, over and over, to 'relocate' to an upper-floor lounge. People walked into the Tremont lobby, looked at the command center, and took a quick powder. Ellen and Nick Palladino were in the bar; Wayne had mustered a volunteer force of fifteen schoolmates to take their own cars and cruise the cemetery, the parking lot of the school, Hester Park. Beth had overheard a cop tell another that it was like bumper cars out there, but that no one had the heart to stop them.

Supporting Beth under one arm, Pat brought her to a more comfortable chair by the piano. Candy Bliss followed. She wanted a picture of Ben for distribution to the media. It was getting

74

late now, and she didn't want to miss morning paper deadlines.

Did Beth have a picture? She had dozens — she'd brought a score of them for purposes of bragging, for the reunion.

But she had no idea, she told Captain Bliss, where her purse was.

Pat found it under the luggage trolley. It was wet, the contents half-scattered. He held out a picture of Ben in his baseball shirt, grinning with his Velcroed catch mitt held close to one cheek.

Beth would wonder later, What had she been imagining? Had she believed, as very small children do, that because Ben was out of her vicinity, was invisible to her, he had in fact been suspended in a pocket of the universe? That he sat on a bubble, safe but estranged, waiting for his mother to notice him again, so he could resume being real? Had Beth believed that because she, his own mother, could not see him, Ben had stopped existing as a complete being who could feel terror and bewilderment?

Ben was a real child in the urban night.

"Ben!" Beth screamed. And again, as the fragile crust of her muddled restraint cracked and then broke entirely, "Ben! Ben! Ben! Ben!" It got easier. "Ben!" Beth screamed. "Ben!" When Pat put his hand over her arm to try to ease her down, she leaned over and seized it in her teeth, biting hard, drawing blood. The room took on the aspect of a hospital emergency room, a sudden bustle. Pat and Jimmy tried to strong-arm Beth; but she tossed them off as they scrabbled to grab different parts of her. She was an eel, a thing coated with resistant gel. The manager ran for the purple security guards, who watched in pity as Beth thrashed, blocking her path to the door every time she got to her feet. She was strong, famously strong. She noticed everything: Pat's bleeding hand; the fearful, furtive glances; the looking away of the departing couples who had to pass through the lobby. She saw Nick with his shiny charcoal-brown head of curls in his hands; she thought he might be crying. His back was heaving up and down. Beth stopped stock-still for a deep breath, and then she screamed again, "Ben! Ben! Ben!"

Candy Bliss told the manager tersely, "Call a doctor."

"I don't know a doctor," said the formal, chubby manager.

"Well, don't you have an emergency physician on call to the hotel?"

"We've never had . . . What does she want?"

"You simple — " said Candy Bliss, letting out stored breath in a huff. "Shit. Call 911."

Beth was wearying; her arm muscles burned. But she only had to look at the bright banquet of children's photos — primary-colored, gleaming — on the coffee table and she would feel the scream percolate up again, as impossible to resist or contain as an orgasm. "Ben! Ben! Ben!"

The manager brought Candy Bliss a portable phone. "The mother is having trouble . . . Yes, exhausted . . . Yes, you can hear her . . . Well, no, not a transport . . . Send someone out."

"Christ God, Beth, please stop!" her father told her firmly.

"Ben!" she screamed at his heavy, veined face. He looked like a hound, sad-eyed and pouching. A bluff, once-handsome man, features blurred by years of gin gimlets. "Beeeeennnnn!" Tears formed in Bill's eyes. Pat was repelled — shivering, he backed away from the couch where Beth struggled.

Beth looked at the clock. It was blurred. Could it be eleven? She screamed, "Beeeennnn!"

A paramedic, very cute, slipped a blood-pressure cuff around Beth's arm. And the doctor who arrived, minutes later, in a jogging suit, squirted golden liquid out of a syringe; the drops flicked down. "We need to get you some rest, here," he told her, swabbing parts of her arms and hands with alcohol, whatever patches of skin he could reach as she flailed. "Listen," he said to the room at large, "we need — "

Nick charged across the room then and half-lay on top of Beth; he smelled wonderful, spicy. His chest was harder than Pat's, bigger. He held her left arm against her body while the paramedic extended the right. The shot was painful, stinging, aching as it seeped in. "Bethie," said Nick. "I know, I know."

"What the fuck?" Beth said, laughing. "You don't know. *I* don't even know."

The medicine was spreading her legs, stilling her chest, compressing her jaw; she felt a line of saliva gather at the corner of her mouth. It was anesthetic. "You can operate now," she told the doctor; he didn't know it was her small joke.

And then black wings brushed her face. And fell.

When Beth awoke, she was tucked hard into a huge bed. Tucked so hard she was nearly straitjacketed.

Ben.

Every available light in the room was on. Directly beside her, in a second king-sized bed, Pat was asleep on top of the bedspread. "Pat?" she whispered. He was oblivious, snoring.

Beth had to pee. She got up, danced sideways for a step, then made her way into the lush, cream-tiled bathroom. She peed, steady, calm, purged, as if the medicine had deadened a section of brain stem. She wanted to brush her teeth. I am doing the things people do, Beth thought, still wanting to eliminate my body's wastes, clean myself, quench my thirst. Unbidden, Beth thought how even when her mother died, she and Ellen were stunned, not that life went on, but how quickly life went on, and how unchanged it was. People could not wait to eat or to get a newspaper. The young priest had told Beth this eating, this talking, these were affirmations of life. He was the humanist kind; he thought he could trick people into Catholicism by pretending the program had been revamped. Beth knew very well, back then, that she did not want to affirm her life and health. She knew that even more securely now. She simply wanted to be shed of bodily urgencies. She forced open a window crosshatched with wire, and craned her neck up and out. There was an alley down there, narrow, and a wall, the other wing of the hotel, that went up farther than Beth could see. A cat was down there, stirring among the dumpsters. Beth tapped the glass; the cat looked up. She saw its gold eyes snap and its maniacal grin. She did not feel Ben, neither his death or his reaching. She slammed the window closed. Pat gargled a snore. You dumb boy, she thought, looking at him. I don't like you.

Opening the closets, cracking the drawers, she found no luggage. Nothing of hers. She could not find a clock. Pat winced in his sleep.

Beth looked out into the corridor. It was absolutely hushed, dim-lighted. She could not find her shoes. Faintly, from outside, she could hear the whump of beating helicopter blades.

Down in the elevator, in the lobby — it was lighter, but still. At the desk, a young blond woman slumbered on her cupped hand. When Beth approached, she sat up and stifled a little shriek.

"Where are the police?" Beth asked her.

"Oh," said the clerk, instantly sympathetic. "They left."

"They left?"

"Well, that is, they didn't *leave* — there are a lot of them outside. But they took the phones and stuff down and went back to the station." She brightened up. "Channel Five was here. And Seven — Eyewitness News. They set up stuff right here in the lobby for the ten o'clock news. But the lady police chief wouldn't let them wake you up."

Beth nodded.

"I need my things."

"Ah, toothpaste? A toothbrush? I can get you one."

"No, my own things. My bag."

"I think it's locked up." The young clerk pawed through a ring of keys, found Beth's duffel, handed it over to her. Beth dragged it to a washroom off the lobby. She removed her reeking shirt and pulled on a T-shirt over her jeans. She found a cotton sweater, bright with red and gold beads. For the luncheon on Sunday. Red shiny flats. She put all of it on. Bodily urgencies. She washed her face and brushed her teeth. As she shoved the toilet articles back into the bag, she saw Ben's clothes tumbled among her own underwear, and Kerry's tiny tights, her footie pajamas. Ben's rubber sandals. His Blackhawks jersey. She was such a bad, haphazard packer. Beth zipped her duffel and lay down on it, her forehead on the tile floor.

Then she rose, lugged the duffel back out to the counter.

"I have to go out," she told the clerk.

"Do you want me to call someone? Your friend — " she glanced at a clipboard in front of her — "Ms. DeNunzio?"

"I just have to go out."

"It's the middle of the night. No stores are open."

Ben had been missing more than twelve hours. This girl thought Beth wanted to go shopping. The girl asked, "Do you want a coffee?"

Beth said, "No thank you," and walked out

80

into the night, which was balmy, Floridian, cleansed.

A half-dozen squads ranged around the circle drive in a loose ring, including a van Beth assumed from the array of electronic plumage on top housed a portable communications center. Cables snaked from the van across the sidewalk, under and through the doors of the Tremont. The fabled Eyewitness News truck was still there as well, its white-eyed lights giving the whole dark stretch of pavement an Oscar-night feel; and a group of what Beth assumed to be print journalists were talking with one of the young detectives. *They* were talking, but he was just smiling and shaking his head. She watched the photogs, their arms draped with the heavy groceries of their profession, lining up to shoot the squad cars under the arch that said 'Tremont Hotel'. Boring stock shot, Beth thought; that should be me taking it. Or I should be in it, to make the shot better. She crossed behind the van, and not a single person seemed to notice her passing.

Out on the quiet street, street lamps — the hazy, muted halogen kind her father put so much stock in — threw the only illumination.

Ben. A moonless night.

Looking across the street, Beth could see the blue roof lights of Immaculata. There was no traffic to dodge. Beth crossed the street, growing stronger on gulps of air. She peered into the door of C Building. Inside, all was darkness. Think of C Building, she told herself — that's something that won't hurt if you think about it.

In C Building, the juniors and seniors would congregate before school. A sophomore could come in if she was dating a junior guy; but these miscegenetic relationships were barely tolerated. Beth could see the door to the student council office — the door for which Beth, as an officer, had her own key. She and Nick would draw the curtains after third lunch, lock the door, and lie on the meeting table, sweating and probing. All through the afternoon's trigonometry and English III, Beth's stomach would ache and contract. She had believed then that everyone who looked at her knew, could see Nick's handprints on her as if they had been impressed with luminous paint.

She walked through the courtyard, past the statue, past the marquee that read 'See "Dracula!" at Olde Tyme Dramatics' and 'Welcome Home Immaculata Class of '70!' Out past the field house, the tennis courts, out to the field.

Just before the gate to the bleachers, she crossed the red wooden bridge that spanned a tributary of Salt Creek. For a generation, village engineers had tried to dam the little stream; in spring, its swollen overrun made the football field a slippery marsh. Nothing worked. The creek always re-established its course. The bridge was so defaced with carvings the paint was virtually nonexistent. It looked red only from a distance. Teenagers from years that followed Beth's own youth, teenagers more skilled at tagging with a spray-paint can, had scrawled ominous messages: 'Men of the 2-and-2, Arise!'

'Spick Power Rules!' There were also the usual romantic epitaphs: 'Justin Smashed My Heart', 'Christine Blows Ryan'.

Beth once would have swung herself down, briefly, to see whether the heavily etched marks that proclaimed 'Steven and Ellen 4-Ever More' were still there. '4-Ever' had not even spanned junior year; Ellen later said Steven Barrett's band-major lips made her flesh creep, though it had taken her six months to decide that it wasn't her fault. But Beth knew the carving remained, a chestnut. Tonight, instead of looking, Beth stood over the stream, no more than half a foot deep, intent on seeing a clue.

But she knew she needn't look for Ben here.

Ben would not willingly go near water. 'It is impossible,' the YMCA instructor once wrote to Beth, 'to evaluate Benjamin's progress at swimming because he refuses to get into the water.' When they swam, even in a bright, shallow pool, Ben attached himself to Beth's waist like a python. He would relax his legs and kick near the steps, with tentative joy. But if Beth walked out farther, even if the water was only up to her ribcage, he would brace himself around her, seem to want to meld into her. A solid, sloppy swimmer who loved water, Beth could not imagine the origins of this fear — had she ever terrified the children with drowning tales? Held them under for a panicky instant, intended for a tease? Never, not ever. There had been that one time when Ben fell off the pier at Lake Delavan. But hadn't her brother snatched Ben out of the water instantly, almost before his face got wet? With Beth screaming like a Comanche the whole time at Vic to be more careful . . . Vincent swam with quicksilver efficiency, had since he was four. Even baby Kerry now struggled to get out of Pat's arms and paddle.

When they visited Pat's aunt in Florida, Vincent ran into the waves; Pat had to chase him and explain the undertow. Ben would not even walk on the damp sand. "There is too much water," he told Beth, solemnly.

"Ben," she had coaxed him then, "come in, just a little. Mama will hold you."

Ben, stolid in his neon-pink trunks, pointed. "Is that the deep end?" His terror was like a scent on him. He didn't even trust Beth to get too close to him, as if she would overwhelm him and rush him into the water. Beth thought, back then, he's hostage to us — to people so large we could compel him to do almost anything. She could not remember ever being so small, vulnerable, so dependent on goodwill.

"There's no deep end of the ocean, Ben," she told him gently. "That's the shore. And it goes on and on, all along here, for miles. You have to go out and out a long way before it gets deep. That's way out there, where the boats go."

"So this is the three feet?" Ben persisted.

"Not even that, Ben. It's not even as deep as a pool, along the edge here. Look, it isn't even up to Vincent's knees."

"I don't want to go in the deep end of the

ocean," Ben told her. "Sharks are there. Do I have to go?"

"No, no, Benbo," Beth had said, scooping him up, unsure whether she should just stomp out there and dip him, get it over with. She didn't want her boy to grow up timid, shy of this, of that. "Don't be afraid. I would be with you. Mama would never let the ocean snatch you away. I would hold you tightest and tightest, wouldn't I?"

"You know what?" Ben told her then, buying time. "You can go to the deep end. You can go there. You just start walking, until it goes over your head and then you keep on walking on the bottom. But then if you want to go back, that's too hard because the water just rubs all the, all the . . . "

"What, Ben?"

"All the feet marks away. You can't ever turn around and go back. You can't find it." And Beth, chilled, sat with him, all that long afternoon, high on the brow of the beach, scooping sand.

Bracing herself on her hands, Beth climbed to the top deck of the bleachers. They were slippery with dew, tacky with chipped paint. She held her arms and shivered. Wind from the cloudy sky seemed to reach down for her. Hunt. Prod. Beth lay on the bleachers, stretching herself out to fullest length, and emptied herself of tears, until the shoulders of her sweater were soaked, and her forehead pulsed against the wood.

When she looked up, not at a sound, but at something else, a disturbance of the air, Candy

85

Bliss was standing at the foot of the bleachers. She held a plastic zip bag, small enough for a sandwich. In it was Ben's high-topped shoe, so clean and new the red parrot still glowed in the dark.

4

FINDING the tennis shoe changed everything.

It was the shoe that made Ben kidnapped. It proved for Candy Bliss that Ben had not wandered away on his own.

The knowledge that her child was in a stranger's hands should have accelerated her panic, but in fact it seemed to slow Beth down.

The shoe, Candy explained, had been found on a low shelf in the newsstand, low enough that Ben could have put it there himself. But it was tied neatly in a tight bow, in a way that most three-year-olds could never have done alone; and he could not have taken it off without untying it, either. "It's not conclusive, Mrs. Cappadora," said Candy Bliss. "But it's enough to start on. And, of course, that's how we felt anyway."

"That someone abducted Ben?"

Candy nodded. "It just . . . that whole lobby full of people. You know, hiding in plain sight . . . " She shook her head. "Beth, now, you're sure Ben couldn't tie?"

"God no. He could barely cut pancakes with a fork. He was three." She snagged her lip with her teeth. "He's three."

"Well, I'm never sure. I mean, I'm close to my nephew, but you have to live in the same house to really commit all those developmental stages to memory. And this is my first . . . "

"Your first?"

"My first case involving a child so young. Of this kind."

"I see. Other kinds?" Beth asked.

"Well, in Tampa I used to work juvenile. Back when I started, that's what a female officer in the South did. And later . . . "

"Later?"

"Well, homicide."

"I see. You don't have children of your own?" Beth asked, amazing herself at her even-measured voice, because she knew that if she looked behind her, she could see herself galloping back and forth across the verge of the parking lot, under the moon, keening and shuddering.

"I don't," said Candy. "I . . . kind of wish I did."

"Maybe soon," Beth said, thinking, For Christ's sake, what are we talking about?

"Uh, well, I think not. I'm thirty-six. Maybe. Anyhow, he can't tie, and you can see how this bow looks." Beth stared at her son's tiny shoe as if it were a chip of meteor, an extraterrestrial phenomenon.

The service door swung wide as they approached, a young officer anticipating them from a cue Beth couldn't discern. She walked blinking into the sharp light reflecting off the stainless-steel expanses of sinks and stoves and straight into the muzzle of two huge and straining dogs.

"McGinty!" cried Candy, as if she'd just

found her long-lost brother. But the barrel-chested, red-haired uniform cop was looking at Beth.

"Mrs. Cappadora," he said softly. "This is Holmes and this is Watson." The bloodhounds sat down, respectfully enough, at a silent gesture from McGinty's right hand. "We call them the bionic noses. We scented them off your little boy's shoe . . . and they got as far as the parking lot. We scented them again, and they went straight to the same place, to a spot in the parking lot a little west of the front entrance. We assume the car was there . . ."

"The car that belonged to whoever it was who took Ben," said Candy.

"I know what he meant," Beth snapped. "I'm not stupid. I was a newspaper photographer for years." Candy nodded, tight-lipped. Pat showed up then, his face blurred with sleep, his hand still seeping under the bandage from Beth's bite, and Candy sat down with both of them. After the state troopers assigned to the case arrived, they would expand their survey of mapped coverage areas for ground and air searches. There would be computer searches, with the help of the list provided by the reunion planners, and the first individuals they would concentrate on interviewing would be those with criminal histories.

"Criminal histories?" Pat asked. "Kids from Immaculata?"

"Not kids anymore," said Candy. "And yeah, in any group that big there's a fair chance we're going to turn up some people, maybe spouses,

89

with histories involving — " They both looked at Beth, and Candy continued, "Abuse. Or assault. Or something."

"With children?" Beth asked.

"Maybe."

"Like?"

"Like, for example, your friend Wayne. Beth, there was a statutory offense, involving a juvenile, in the seventies."

"Wayne is as close to my children as their blood uncles. Wayne would never hurt Ben. This is because he's gay . . . "

"Which is what I thought, Beth, and it turned out that the kid was sixteen and he was nineteen, and it was probably just a romance that got some parents all juiced . . . see? Most of these things turn out to be nothing, but we check them all . . . "

Ellen wandered into the kitchen, zeroed in on Beth, and enfolded her. In sweats and a ponytail, Ellen looked reduced, frail and young. She held Beth against her as Candy explained that it would be wise to get the parents' lie detector tests out of the way. They could visit the technician today or wait until Monday.

"You think Beth arranged for Ben to be stolen?" Ellen asked.

"No, but most kidnappings are domestic in origin. They're custody-related, or they turn out to be problems with relatives or former caregivers," Candy Bliss explained.

There were lists and interviews and the first Crimestopper poster of Ben's face to approve; Beth — luckily, she thought — looked away at the last minute, so she never saw Ben's trusting eyes look back at her from the black-and-white photocopy. Ellen helped Beth take a bath, drawing Beth's jeans down over her hips, handing her into the tub as she would have helped a brittle-boned grandmother. While Beth lay in the water and Pat paced, smoking, in the bedroom, the phone rang almost incessantly. Ellen would answer, crisply, "She's asleep," or "No, they've lived in Madison more than ten years." Dressed in Ellen's clean clothes, so long on her she looked like Nellie Forbush in her sailor suit in *South Pacific*, Beth sat in front of the mirror and dried her own hair. Some time in the late afternoon, Officer Taylor asked her what she remembered about her classmate Sean Meehan. His second child had died four years before, a crib death that never felt quite right. When Beth began to dry-heave in the sink, the doctor, whose name Beth never knew, showed up again and gave her sample packets of tranquilizers. But when she couldn't keep those down, either, he gave her another shot; and she slept, hearing everything, even her brother Bick's voice — she tried to wake up to talk. to Bick, but couldn't fight her way through the slumberous layers. At one point, Pat sat her up and they watched a grainy, early-morning news video of teams of neighborhood volunteers and Immaculata classmates walking the forest preserve and the golf course shoulder to shoulder. When Ben's baseball-cap picture flashed on the screen and a young woman said, "A community is mobilized to find little Ben," Beth screamed and Pat turned the set off.

A bellman from the Tremont staff brought up a tray of cheese cubes and fruit, with a card tucked in it that reminded them they ate compliments of the Tremont, part of the nationwide chain of Hospitality Hotels. Ellen forced Beth to eat grapes and a single cube of cheese. Coffee materialized. Beth drank four cups.

It was still light when Candy came up into Beth's room and asked her if she was ready to talk to the press.

Beth said, "Of course not."

Candy winced. "Well, you don't have to. But I want you to if you can. You don't have to talk to a bunch of reporters, just one. I have one picked out. She's okay. And you *could* talk to everybody. You could talk to Channel Five, Seven, Two, Nine . . . the *Tribune*, the local paper, the *Sun-Times*. They're all here."

"I don't want to talk to anybody. Let Pat talk. He's a good talker."

"But Beth, you're the mother. People respond to mothers. They see your emotion."

"You want me to cry in front of these people."

"No, I don't want you to perform," Candy said.

The sedative's still-warm brandy in her blood made Beth bold. "I'm not the crying-in-front-of-other-people type," she said.

"You are so," Ellen put in.

"If I was," said Beth, "I'm not anymore. This

is my kid, *my* kid . . . " Beth felt the nausea crest and recede. "You don't understand."

"No," said Candy. "I don't. But I understand how far-reaching these reports can be, and how many people watch, and how we can get their eyes working for us."

"Look," Ellen told Beth. "You are going to do this. You are going to do this because it's one thing you can do to help find Ben. Now, sit up and get ready."

"I look like a sack of shit."

"That's okay," said Candy, and Beth thought, remembering her newspaper days, yes, of course, this is a tableau: the grieving mother she had herself photographed five or ten times, eyes dreadful with sleep deprivation, cheekbones like rocky ridges. "But you don't want to look frightening," Candy went on, "or they'll think . . . "

"They'll think what?"

"That you're nuts and you did it," said Ellen as she went to get her makeup bag. Candy watched as she smoothed Beth's hair back and secured it with a gold clip.

"Put on a little eye shadow, Beth," Ellen said. Beth stared at the pot of greens and blues and beiges.

"Let me do that," Candy suddenly said briskly. "I'm very good at makeup." And, Beth would later reflect, more times than she could ever imagine why, Candy really *was* good at it: the discreet taupe orbs she sketched under Beth's brows made her look wan but not wild; the minimal amount of cover-up she applied did

93

not hide the pouches that flanked Beth's nose, but muted them.

"Now, what I'm going to do," Candy explained, brushing gently, "is bring Sarah Chan up here with her crew. And we'll do her first, because she's on deadline, and they troubled to send an anchor, and Channel Two is the top-watched news. And then if you want to do anybody else, you can — they're all going to have reports anyhow. There will be a lot of lights, Beth." Beth thought briefly of a gynecological exam, of her doctor telling her the patient litany, 'Now, I'm going to insert the speculum . . . ' She interrupted Candy.

"I know about lights, I'm a photographer."

"Okay. And all you'll have to do is answer her questions. They're taping, so if you need to go back over something, if you're nervous — "

"I'm not *nervous*," Beth said, more violently than she meant; she didn't need to compel Candy to despise her, too. "Can I see the press release?" she asked then, trying to sound helpful, even sane. Someone went to get a copy and Beth scanned it; it was not lyric prose: 'No witnesses as yet to the disappearance . . . several promising leads . . . a full-scale investigation.'

"You don't mention the shoe," Beth said.

"And we're not," Candy told her. "That's our hole card. Only one person, probably one, knows why that shoe was there. We'll never get anything physical off the canvas, like — "

"Like fingerprints?"

"Right. But that's what we'll use for the confessors."

94

"Confessors."

"The people who say they took Ben, when they call."

"People will call?"

"Oh, they have, Beth. They already have. There are chronics out there who just want the attention, and maybe some people who are genuinely guilty of something and so tormented they have to confess to something else. They all come out of the woodwork, Beth."

And Beth locked on an image of a darkened room, a moon-pale face with a phone receiver clutched tight next to it, speaking quietly, whispering, perhaps afraid someone in the next room would hear . . . and then Sarah Chan, slim as a pleat and fragrant in her blue suit, knocked at the door and the room filled with a bristle of cables and light poles. Pat sat down next to Beth on the sofa.

"Touch her," said Candy. And Pat placed his arm along the back of the sofa, resting it just shy of Beth's shoulders.

"Mrs. Cappadora," said Sarah Chan, "I want you to know that all of us want to do everything we can to help find your little boy. You know how these things are. They really draw people together. A whole city will be praying for Brian — "

"Ben."

"For Ben. I'm very sorry about that. I just got here and I haven't really brought myself entirely up to speed."

Beth couldn't say anything.

"Mrs. Cappadora?" Sarah Chan prodded.

"I understand," Beth gulped, finally.

She suddenly recalled a moment from her newspaper days — shooting a family whose only son, a teenager, had died hours before in one of those hideous northern Wisconsin county-trunk car wrecks. All at once the boy's old grandmother said loudly, "Oh, well, we used to do the same thing. My husband and his buddies would have a big tin bucket of beer on the floor in the back of the car, and they'd drive up and down raising hell. Oh, my yes, we did. They all do it." Beth was dumbstruck, her fingers fumbling with her old Hasselblad (the editor wanted mournful portraits, not news shots). Was she supposed to agree: kids will be kids, kids will be incinerated in old Chevys?

Sarah Chan's breezy reference to 'how these things are' stunned Beth in exactly the same way, she realized, but now she was on the other end of the lens.

"Mrs. Cappadora, are you ready?" asked Sarah Chan.

"Let Pat talk," Beth pleaded.

"We agreed," Ellen told her firmly. "I'll be right here."

And so the tech attached a necklace mike to Beth's shirt and did a sound check.

"Mrs. Cappadora, before we begin," said Sarah Chan, "I know I shouldn't be asking you this, but if you could manage not to talk to other media, I think this might have a great deal more impact."

"Get over yourself, Sarah," said Candy in a warning tone. And the videographer, a young

96

woman in tight jeans and a huge Harvard sweatshirt, trained the lens on Sarah Chan.

"We're here in the room of the Tremont Hotel in Parkside where the Cappadora family waits and wonders and grieves," she said. "Less than twenty-four hours ago . . . "

"Sarah," Candy said. "Do the stand-up later. Let's get this over with."

Abruptly, Sarah Chan sat down next to Beth and Pat on the sofa. "Now, remember, we'll be taping, so if you feel as though you haven't said exactly what you want to say, we can always stop and start over," she told Beth soothingly.

And then she changed, became glowing, her face that of a veritable madonna of empathy. "Beth and Pat, this is the town where you grew up. Could you ever have imagined that something like this could happen in Parkside, in a lobby filled with all your friends from high school?"

"What kind of question is that?" Pat asked, and Chan made a tiny cutting gesture to the photog. "I mean, of course not. This is a small town. Beth and I grew up with these people. We know these streets like the back of our hand."

"But the possibility still exists that someone you know actually took your little boy," Sarah Chan said sorrowfully, gesturing for the tape to roll again.

"It exists, but I don't believe it's possible," said Pat in what Beth considered his best Scout voice. "Whatever has happened to Ben didn't have anything to do with Immaculata."

"Mrs. Cappadora . . . Beth," Sarah Chan

asked then, "your feelings now must be unimaginable . . . ."

Beth said, "Yes."

"I mean, the combination of fear and wondering how long it will take, the grief . . . " Beth stared at the line of thin pancake that bisected Sarah Chan's face neatly at the neck, like a mask, and said nothing. The reporter tried again: "We really have no idea how you must be feeling tonight, the second night — "

"You really have no idea," Beth agreed.

"So," said Sarah Chan patiently, "is there anything you would like to ask our viewers, the people of Chicagoland, who care deeply about your loss?"

Beth sat silently.

"Beth?" Sarah Chan urged her.

"Yes," Beth said. "I want to say something to the person who took my son Ben from this hotel lobby." Please have mercy on me, Beth thought. Please have an ounce of human heart and bring me my baby, she thought. I beg you to spare him, she thought, and said, "It's that . . . it's that I don't expect you to bring Ben back." Sarah Chan gasped audibly, and even the photographer jumped. Beth felt Pat cringe from her, as if he'd been stung.

But Candy Bliss held up her hand, as if to hold back traffic, and Beth looked straight and long into her eyes. As long as she watched Candy's unblinking blue eyes, she knew with an utter certainty that she could continue. And so she did.

"I don't expect you to bring Ben back, because

98

you are a sick, heartless bastard."

"Mrs. Cappadora," Sarah Chan breathed. "Beth . . . "

"I don't expect you to bring Ben back because if you could do this thing, you either don't understand the nature of the hell we are going through, or you don't care."

She cleared her throat. "So, I am not going to appeal to you. But anyone else . . . anyone who sees Ben's face, and who has a heart, you know that whoever is with Ben is not me or Pat. It's not his mom or dad. So if you could, what I want you to do is, grab Ben. If you have to hurt the person, that's okay. I will reward you; my family will reward you; my friends will reward you. We will give you everything we have." Beth paused. "That's all," she said.

Sarah Chan looked up at Candy. "We can't use this," she said in dismay.

Evenly, Candy asked, "Why not?"

"Because it . . . because it's not . . . I mean, pardon me, Mr. and Mrs. Cappadora, but if somebody really does have the little boy and they hear this, it's going to just infuriate . . . No one expects her to say — "

"You're afraid that people are going to dislike Beth because she's angry at the guy who took her baby? Because she doesn't want to beg a kidnapper? You think she's not sympathetic enough?"

"It's not that . . . " said Sarah Chan.

Candy pressed one finger against her forehead. "These are your choices, Sarah. Either you use that or you get nothing else. And I will go downstairs and get Walter Sheer or Nancy Higgins or whoever else I see in the lobby, and Beth can say the same thing again, and they will use it, and they will have this exclusive and you will not."

"Detective, I don't see why . . . "

Candy stood behind Beth and placed her hands over Beth's head. They felt to Beth like a cap of benediction. "Because she told the truth, is why," said Candy Bliss.

5

ON Monday afternoon, over Beth's objections, Pat insisted they leave the Tremont. Though she could not begin to tell him why, she knew that the close heat and the cooking smells, the family-funeral atmosphere of Italian coming and going that would permeate her in-laws' house could strangle her. If that was possible, it would be more unbearable than the hotel, which was, while terrifying, at least muffled and anonymous. You didn't bump up against someone you owed something to every five seconds.

But Pat was resolute; this was stupid. She had not seen Vincent or Kerry in nearly two days. Pat wanted to be with his parents and his sisters. "And I have to tell you, Bethie, I think you'll get more of a grip if we go home to my mother's. You'll . . . come around a little," he said. "Every minute we sit here, we're just looking at where it happened."

And so they walked to the car, the manager following them out onto the sidewalk and across the parking lot, explaining more than once that, of course, there would be no charge for their stay, and that the management of the Tremont, and indeed all Hospitality Hotels everywhere (everywhere in the galaxy, thought Beth), was deeply sorry for their ordeal, as if their rest had been disturbed by a noisy air conditioner.

Reporters followed the manager, some actually calling out questions: Had there been any word from the kidnappers? Did the FBI have any serious suspects? Beth had never understood before how people besieged by press people managed to ignore their insistence, especially under conditions of enormous stress.

She knew now. You did not hear them. They were not even annoying, like black flies. Angelo had said that the phone rang all day at his house, reporters trying, as they explained, to expand on the 'family perspective'. A police officer stationed at the Cappadoras' usually simply took the telephone, explained politely that no one in the house could comment on an ongoing investigation, and hung up. When Angelo and Rosie's Golden Hat catering trucks left their store on Wolf Road, news vans sometimes trailed after the drivers. Even as Beth got into the car, a young writer from *People* magazine was putting a business card into her hand and literally closing Beth's fingers over it, telling her that *People* had a reputation for caring, exactitude, and results. "Talking to us will get the word out in every airport and drugstore in America," she warned Beth. "So call me." Beth nodded, closing the door and locking it, rolling up the window. She crushed the card and pushed it into the ashtray.

And yet, she thought, press, police, or family — after all, what did it matter? People could move their mouths at her if they wished. She was not, anymore, real. She was a faux woman, a toupee human. She was already putting into place her cloak of invisibility, tucking the edges of dark cloth around her mind to screen out information and light. She could go to her in-laws' house, or Madison, or Amarillo, or Uranus. She would find neither stimulus nor peace.

Pat had accused her, softly, of being 'spaced out'. His own face was rough with an eruption of hives; he stank of smoke; his hair was oily. When he lay down to sleep, he cried out. Beth offered him her drugs to shut him up, but Pat said he needed to be alert, to help the police any way he could. Beth thought otherwise. The only way she could help the police or anyone was by standing far enough from herself to deflect idiocy, the strong urge to slobber and gibber and scratch.

As they stepped into the living room from Angelo and Rosie's front porch, Vincent threw himself on Pat, and Beth held him briefly, stroking his hair. Jill presented Kerry to Beth to cuddle and feed; but when Pat saw that Beth did not notice when the bottle became disengaged from the baby's mouth, he took her and fed her himself, until she fell asleep. Pat's sister Monica made pot after pot of coffee and could not pass the piano without playing a few bars of something. His sister, Teresa, simply asked everyone who came through the door, "What are we going to do?" until Pat, sharply, told her to stop. Beth sat in a huge wing chair just inside the door, and everyone who passed her, coming into the house, seemed about to genuflect. The Comos came, and Wayne Thunder, twice, and a dozen of Angelo's business friends, who brought fruit in baskets and pans of lasagne, though Wayne said that bringing lasagne to Rosie's was even more egregious than coals to Newcastle.

Neither Beth nor her brothers had been able to eat lasagne since their mother's death, when it had seemed for months that the lasagne in the freezer was like the loaves and fishes — that it would never be gone, was breeding on its own. They had given lasagne to the mailman, to strangers collecting for environmental organizations, to the families of school friends.

But Rosie now accepted each new offering with effusive grace. "We haven't had any time to cook — how kind," she would say in wonder, when in fact Rosie had done nothing but cook since Saturday morning, obsessively, serving full meals to whoever was in the house, and, even now, in the hot center of a June afternoon, had turned up the air conditioning so that she could bake pork chops with peas and tomatoes in the oven without causing anyone to stroke.

Just before dinner, when Rosie was elaborately setting the table in the formal dining room with its mirrored wall, Beth heard Angelo in the kitchen talking with another man, an unfamiliar voice. Something tripped an alarm in her, and she got up and walked around the end of the hall, until she stood just inside the door of the bathroom next to the east kitchen wall.

He saw her anyway.

"Charley," said Beth.

"Bethie honey," said the man, who wore an immaculate white shirt, red tie, and blue pinstripe with an almost undetectable thread of crimson. "Bethie honey, I swear to God. I swear to God. What is this world?" He held her against him, and in spite of herself Beth felt that unmistakable surrender to the embrace of an Italian man her father's age, the feeling that you had managed to crawl onto shore and been cut on the sharp stones, but everything would be all right as soon as you got some dry clothes on.

She didn't know his real name. Yes, Beth suddenly thought, she did know it. Ruffalo. His daughter was named Janet. Charley Ruffalo. But she had never called him anything except Charley Two, though of course not to his face, because he said everything twice. In some obscure, village-linked way, he was related to Angelo — they called each other 'cousin' — and Charley ran what Pat lovingly called the most profitable single-truck delivery company in the Northern Hemisphere. "Bethie," he said now. "I've been doing my best. I've been doing my best. I've talked with some guys. And Bethie, Angie, I swear to God, I swear to God, there's nothing. There's nothing out there."

He meant, Beth knew — and Angelo knew she knew — that Ben had not been taken by professional criminals.

"Thank you, Charley," she said, and heard Angelo take a breath, sharply. They spoke in Italian. Charley kissed Beth, his cheek soft as a leather glove soaked in Aramis.

"Eat," said Rosie, with not even a trace of her usual vigor. Everyone sat down. Vincent ate heartily, and so did the current Parkside cop in residence, a black kid named Cooper, but none of the other adults, so far as Beth could observe, did anything but cut up their chops. Teresa's husband, Joey, finally threw down his napkin and stormed away from the table, Teresa bustling after him, casting back an apologetic look at her mother. In the middle of the nondinner, Bick showed up to tell Beth that their older brother, Paul, who'd just returned from a business trip, was on his way. "I didn't know what to tell him, Bethie," Bick said. "Is there any news that isn't on the news?"

From the rim of her eye, Beth saw the young cop stiffen. But she said in her mind, This is my brother, fool, a lawyer, not a gossip columnist, and said aloud, "They found his shoe. They found Ben's shoe in the newsstand."

Bick held her again. "So they think someone has him?"

"They think someone has him."

"So did the local cops call the FBI?"

And so Pat explained the complexities of kidnapping law, as best he understood it — Beth was certain he didn't fully understand it — about how it was either a federal crime or it wasn't, depending on whether the kidnapper crossed state lines or air space above state borders or Lake Michigan or an ocean, and that it was a state crime if the kidnapper took the abducted child from one end of California to the other, even by air, and that every state's law on the matter differed slightly. And in the middle of it all, Beth's head began to throb and she went upstairs in search of her drug bottle and fell on Rosie's bed, while in her dreams voices came and went like tide, Candy's and Angelo's and Bick's and, finally, one voice that said, "Mama?"

Beth screamed. She sat up in bed and screamed again. And then Vincent, who stood next to the bed in his T-shirt and underpants, screamed also and burst into tears. Rosie came running down the hall with Monica at her heels and scooped up Vincent, muttering, "*Dormi, dormi*, Vincenzo, sweetheart."

"What the fuck, Beth?" Pat grabbed her arm ungently.

"I thought — I thought it was Ben." He let her go then and cradled the back of her skull in his hand. Ben was their come-into-bed child. Though he fought the process of going to his room, once asleep, Vincent had slept, sprawled, independent and entirely confident, from babyhood. But Ben rarely passed a night without slipping into his parents' room, vaulting his crib bars like a gymnast until Beth took them down in defeat, crawling and then walking into his parents' room, sometimes leaving the sheet between Beth and Pat soaking cold in the morning. "I walk-sleeped," he would explain to them in recent months, since his language had become fluent. It was Ben, also, who called Beth 'Mama', not 'Mom' or 'Ma', as Vincent did. In her sedative blanket, Beth had not recognized Vincent's voice.

Staggering, she got up and made her way down the hall to the guest room. It was the

107

first time in all the years she had known Rosie — basically all the years she could remember — that her mother-in-law had looked at Beth with true scorn. Cradling Vincent, who was falling out of sobs into a hiccuping sleep, she motioned Beth away. Beth walked out onto the terrace off the guest room. Joey and Teresa were staying in there, though evidently they were not yet asleep. There were cars parked all up and down the block, reporters sitting on blankets sipping coffee and Coke from paper cups as if they were at a music festival. They did not see her. There was a Parkside squad parked at the corner of the block, an orange sawhorse set up as a desultory roadblock — as Beth watched, a Channel Nine van drove right around it. Behind her, Joey opened the bedroom door.

"Joey, have you got a butt?" Beth asked.

"Bethie, I didn't know you smoked anymore," Joey, the gentlest of men, told her softly.

"I don't," she told him.

They sat side by side on the terrace and watched the reporters mill, some doing stand-ups for the early broadcasts, their backs to the lighted, entirely presentable shuttered front of Rosie and Angelo's white stone ranch.

"We'll find him, Bethie," Joey said fiercely.

"Oh, Joe," said Beth, putting her arms around him, overcome with tenderness for this kid brother-in-law, tenderness she could not seem to smooth over her own, real little boy, at last asleep again down the hall. And why not?

"Bethie, I would give my right arm, my leg, to find Ben."

108

"I know, honey," she said.

Teresa came out in her nightgown. "I'm pregnant," she said abruptly.

"Jesus fucking Christ on a pony, Tree," her husband hissed, getting up.

"Joey, it's okay. Congratulations, Tree," Beth told her. "*Buona fortuna*. How much?"

"Two months," said Teresa.

"Does Pat know?"

"No. Should I tell him? Rosie knows. She said I shouldn't tell you. I'm sorry I told you. My mouth just opened. I'm crazy in the head, Bethie. We're all crazy."

"I know," said Beth. "Got another butt, Joey?"

After Joey and Teresa lay down on top of the quilt, Beth sat watching the sky drain of darkness. She repeated in her mind the periodic table. Oxygen. Nitrogen. Carbon. Silicon. Sodium. Chlorine. Neon. Strontium. Argon. She knew there were some they hadn't had when she was in high school. Technetium? Californium? Or was she just making that up? The cigarette burned her fingertips. She lay down on the painted wooden floor. Kerry was crying. Someone would feed her.

At eight, Candy came to take Beth and Pat to a lab in Elmbrook for their lie detector tests. Later, Pat told Beth the young technician had made the same speech to both of them: "Relax," he said. "Physically, this will be the least painful thing that ever happens to you. I always tell people to relax, but of course they can't relax, it's a polygraph — who can relax? But it doesn't

109

even really matter if you can't relax, because I'll be able to read your baseline whatever state you're in. And I imagine your state right now is pretty rough. Now, I'm going to start with the question that's the hardest. What's your name?" Both Beth and Pat learned afterward that their answers indicated deception when they were asked if they were responsible for Ben's disappearance.

"That's no biggie," Candy told Beth. "We can always run it again if we have to."

When they got back to Rosie and Angelo's, Ellen was there to drive Beth to the volunteer center in the basement of Immaculata's church hall. Beth asked, "What volunteer center?"

"You know," Ellen said. "Leafleting and searches. This lady came yesterday morning from Crimestoppers and taught us how to set it up. These first seventy-two hours are critical."

There had been three hundred and twenty Immaculata graduates. And there must have been, Pat later said, a hundred and fifty people connected with the school alone in the church hall basement, leaving out the handful of Rosie's neighbors, Bill's lady friend, and the scattering of friends who grew up with Beth's and Pat's sisters and brothers. Nick's wife, Trisha, was there, and all the cheerleaders, and Jimmy Daugherty's wife, and twenty other mothers, classmates, and classmates' wives. There was the principal of Immaculata, the only remaining nun on the whole teaching staff, and four other faculty, including Beth's ancient English teacher, Miss Sullivan, ten years retired. Wayne, whose management training job with AT&T was so intense he estimated he took three days off a year (all Sundays), was there, having canceled all his appointments indefinitely for only the second time in his working life. (The first time, he took a four-week cruise to Australia on a boat with nine hundred other gay men. "We were in the middle of the ocean and I couldn't get a date," he despairingly told Beth later. "I might as well work.") Wayne was in charge of the media, he told Beth. He would screen all requests for interviews and photos and pass on those he thought might advance the search. Even Cecil Lockhart had signed up to come, but then couldn't at the last minute because her mother had taken ill. "But she sends her love, Beth," said Ellen. "And I really believe she meant it. She's going to come and work when her mom gets better. You know, she has a little boy not much older than Ben, from her second marriage — or her third, or her fifth. I didn't even know that, but she sounded so sick over it. Everyone does, Bethie. Everyone."

Just after Beth and Pat arrived, Laurie Elwell walked in, carrying a stack of three-ring binders. She looked as though she had been in bed with flu and shouldn't have gotten up. Since college, Laurie had been Beth's best friend in Madison; she sometimes thought her only friend. She was no more like Beth than the moon is like a hubcap — even as a college freshman, she was cool and self-assured in a way Beth was relatively sure she herself would never be, even as an adult. Laurie was one of those girls who already seemed

111

to know everyone in the financial aid office; presidents of sororities left messages for *her*, not the other way around. Laurie seemed to have been born with an open trunk to the essential information of the universe, and, as the binders proved, she intended to keep it all on file.

Beth and Ellen fought and hung up on one another at least once a year; but Beth's relation to Laurie was as free of the dark underpinnings of childhood and common origin as a summer afternoon. They had met at the time people reinvent themselves, talked each other through the panicky boredom, the manifest prides and fears of parenthood and long marriages.

When Beth saw Laurie and the others, she thought, only for an instant, Now is the time of the reunion. Now I will be able to act.

Beth had said that Laurie could win the Nobel Prize for Organization; and she was in laureate form. The long tables usually used to hold the food at parish teas and wedding breakfasts were covered with phones and stacks of leaflets, posters on red and yellow and blue paper. Pat picked one up, and Beth read the bold-print headline, HAVE YOU SEEN BEN TODAY?, over a thankfully unfamiliar picture of Ben that Ellen had taken last summer in her yard and a phone number Wayne had commandeered for its unforgettability: the numbers spelled out FIND BEN. From one of her notebooks Laurie removed and unfolded a detailed map of the west-side neighborhoods in three panels that, stapled together and tacked up, covered the better portion of one of the walls.

"We'll have a red team, a blue team, and a yellow team," she told Beth and Pat, opening another binder to computer-printed lists she had compiled over the telephone with Wayne and Ellen. "The captains of each team will be responsible for assigning blocks for the team members to leaflet. And then each team will have volunteers here who'll coordinate calls we get from each of the areas."

"When are you going to start leafleting?"

Laurie looked surprised. "Why, now," she said.

"How long can you stay?" Beth asked.

"Well, forever," Laurie told her.

Candy spoke briefly to the assembled volunteers, telling them that every piece of information they gathered was potentially the one nugget of information that could lead them to Ben. "You can't overestimate the importance of your being here, both to Beth and Pat and to us," she said. "You are going to be our eyes and ears in this area for the next few days, and however long or brief the time you can give is valuable time." She told about the shoulder-to-shoulder searches planned for open areas later in the afternoon, and how even those who had to work during the day could join the police in those efforts in the light hours of the early evening. She warned volunteers against attempting to interview residents or to conduct searches on their own. "We have to be one body, with the head of that body right here," she said, turning to Pat. "Pat, do you have anything to add?"

Pat's eyes misted. "Just that we thank you.

113

We thank you. Ben thanks you."

It was Anita Daugherty who stood up and began to applaud, and then everyone else stood and joined in. The peculiarity of the gesture stunned Beth, who turned away and fled for the stairs to the first floor; she supposed it meant encouragement, solidarity. But it sounded like a pep rally, and with volunteers laden with leaflets about to surge up the stairs behind her, she felt like a sick animal in search of a refuge to lie in.

The Chapel of Our Lady opened directly to the right of the altar. There, Beth had taken her flowers to lay in front of the Virgin as a first communicant in her white miniature of a bridal dress. There, she had always believed, she would come as a bride. Now, she wished only that the little sky-blue room with its faded gilt stars on the ceiling had a door to close behind her. Beth knelt and folded her hands. "Hail Mary, full of grace . . . " she said softly. But they were words. They came from nowhere but the back of her throat. In all her life, Beth had felt only twice that she had actually prayed — that is, established a connection between herself and some other consciousness: once in her mother's hospital room shortly after Evie had died; once the day the bleeding stopped, when she'd believed she was miscarrying the pregnancy that turned out to be Ben. For most of the rest of her life, though she knew her Confiteor, her Rosary, her creeds (in Latin at least) as well as she knew the spelling of her name, she had felt outside herself when she said them, even when the linguistic power of the words themselves made her throat close with emotion. "Holy Mary," she whispered again, thinking, If I cannot believe now, if I cannot ask for help now, even given the strong doubt that I would ever be heard except by atmosphere, that I would ever receive anything but the borrowed peace of meditation, if I cannot uncurl my closed hand even a little, I am not deserving of Ben. I have to pray for Ben, she thought. "Holy Mary," she said, the words clicking, dry against the dry roof of her mouth, sounds. "I can't," Beth said.

She smelled Candy before she saw her, smelled the distinct lemony bite that underlay her cologne, like a telegram of cleanliness. The row of blue-velvet-padded kneelers extended a full five feet along a gold rail in front of the white marble folds of the Virgin's gown. A few feet from Beth, Candy knelt, one hand over her eyes.

"Are you Catholic?" Beth asked.

"No," said Candy. "I was just waiting for you."

"There's nothing to wait for," Beth sighed. "I'm done. I never got started. I can't pray."

"My mother always said there's no right way to do it."

"I don't believe."

"In anything?"

"I mean, I don't believe in God."

"Atheist?" asked Candy.

Beth snorted. "No. That takes too much courage."

"Maybe it's faith that really takes the courage.

115

The belief in things unseen."

"Sounds like you were raised Catholic," Beth said.

"Well, I was raised Jewish," Candy told her, standing up. "And there are plenty of comparisons. Guilt. Misogyny. You name it." She reached out her hand and touched the Virgin's marble fingertips. "But some other stuff, too. Like you move the house to take care of someone. You sacrifice everything for a child — and of course you remind the child of that for as long as you live." Candy looked up at the serene face of the Madonna. "She was a Jewish mother, Beth, you know? And if anyone would help you now, maybe it would be a Jewish mother."

"I guess that should be easy to accept right now. They say there are no atheists in foxholes, right?"

"Beth," said Candy, not pausing, "maybe you don't have to believe everything. Maybe you don't have to know how to pray. Maybe you have all you can do right now just to hold on. Maybe holding on is enough."

Beth looked up at the statue of the Virgin. "Hold on, huh?" she whispered. "To what? To *her*?"

"If you want. Maybe."

"And what if there's nothing there?"

"Then . . . you can hold on to me."

6

EVEN Laurie really couldn't stay forever. "I'll come back every weekend until Ben's found," she told Beth, her hand cupping Beth's chin, her eyes fastened unwaveringly on Beth's eyes with Laurie's special earnestness. They both knew she could not come back every weekend — would not — and yet nothing about that reality negated the loving hope that underlay the promise. "There's still a lot more that we can do. Everybody says so. The woman from Crimestoppers says. This week, we'll do the bulk mailings to all the states where every graduate lives now, and they'll be distributed by volunteers there. I'll do a bunch of them from home. By Sunday, we'll have the highway billboard the Firefighters' Association is buying — Bethie, a hundred thousand people are going to see that every day. Jimmy's wife is going to work on that connection with the National Center for Missing and Abused Children. And then there's that TV special coming up, the one called *Missing* — Sarah Chan says we have a very good chance of getting on that, especially now that Ben's been . . . " She stopped.

"Gone so long," Beth finished for her. "Gone so long that the fact of him being gone so long is the story now."

"Oh, God," Laurie said.

It was the end of something. No one would

say it, but they felt the decline, saw it in the faces of the Parkside officers, fewer each day, in the eyes of the volunteers, down after two weeks to a core group of twenty or so. The scent of Barbara Kelliher's Chanel No. 5 had become a kind of leitmotif in Beth's days; it preceded Barbara into the basement room at Immaculata, and behind it would come Barbara's unfailingly strained smile, and the single-minded devotion with which she attached her stack of marked maps and phone messages that had come in the night before. It had occurred to Beth that for a few of the volunteers, the search for Ben was a real labor of love — but not love for her. They hoped, by finding him, to keep lightning from striking their own houses. It was the best, most defensible kind of guilt, the kind that made bystanders jump into freezing water to save collies or derelicts — and thereby save themselves. Beth loved the center, its smell of newly opened reams of medium-weight bond and stale coffee, with a near-romantic fervor. It, and Candy's obsessively cluttered office on the second floor of the Parkside Police Station, were the only places Beth felt sheared, however briefly, of Ben's loss; of the weight she sometimes felt would compress her into a flake of skin.

It was at the center, just after saying goodbye to Laurie, that Beth found out about the tip. A sighting that, unlike others, sounded real. A woman from Minnesota, who refused to leave her name, had called to describe a little boy she had spotted in a shopping center in Minneapolis,

118

walking beside a gray-haired woman in a huge hat and sunglasses. The little boy, she was certain, was Ben. He had been eating a hot dog. It was the hot dog that somehow certified the tip for Barbara. "I think you should go talk to Candy and see if she's going to follow it up," suggested Barbara. "I could drive you."

"I can drive," Beth told her. "Thank you."

She didn't, in fact, have to drive. The car piloted itself into the Parkside Police Station parking lot; she simply had to hang on to the steering wheel. But without quite recognizing why, once she got there she drove out again, the few blocks to Golden Hat Gourmet, where she went into one of the cold cases and got a few cannoli.

Joey, who was working the lunch takeout, wrapped them up for her. "Hungry, Bethie?" he asked hopefully, glancing at Beth's loose jeans, cinched tight with one of Pat's belts. Her hipbones now poked at the pockets like bunches of keys.

"Yep," she told him, stretching her mouth in what she believed still looked like a smile. "Got a cannoli craving, like Tree."

He hugged her, slipped her a Camel, and Beth left, settling the white box with its bowed string beside her in the passenger seat.

No one in the locked offices at Parkside questioned Beth's presence anymore; they simply buzzed her in wordlessly. Though there was an elevator, Beth always took the stairs, and today when she opened the steel door that would lead directly around a corner into Candy's open

119

office, she heard Candy say, " . . . to have somebody go up there and check things out."

"You have to pardon me, Candace," an unfamiliar male voice replied, "but there's no way he's going to free up a team to drive to fucking Minneapolis to talk to some coupon shopper who thought she saw a kid. I mean, Minneapolis? There wasn't one person at that reunion from Minneapolis. There are sixty full-time cops on this department, not six hundred."

"How far the hell away is Minneapolis? People drive all the time, McGuire," Candy said, her voice stiffening. "It's a mobile society."

Beth made herself still to listen.

"Candace, I know how you feel about this, but this kid is dead. This kid is dead, and from his point of view that's probably a good thing, and — "

"Don't say I know it, because I *don't* know it." Beth heard the familiar sound of Candy tapping her eraser on her blotter. "Anyway, this is interstate. I'm going to call Bender."

"And he's going to say, 'Good afternoon, Detective, call me some time in the next century or when hell freezes over.'"

"It's a legitimate alleged sighting across a state line."

"It's just another — " The plainclothes cop, whom Beth had never seen before, turned and noticed her. "Uh, hi, Mrs. Cappadora."

Beth smiled.

"Beth, come in," Candy told her fiercely. "See you later, McGuire." The detective left. "You heard, didn't you." It wasn't a question.

120

"I heard the part about some guy named Bender."

"No, you heard the whole thing. But what you need to know is that this is going to be my excuse to call the FBI, and that's who Bender is — Robert Bender, he's the agent who heads up the bureau in Chicago."

"The FBI," said Beth. "Why?"

"Well, not because we couldn't do the work ourselves," said Candy Bliss. "Though we do have this delicate resource problem. We do have this problem of brass who get fretful if we don't solve a case and get an airtight confession by lunch." She coughed. "But this is supposedly the reason why the FBI exists, to support local jurisdictions involved with federal offenses."

She got up and paced. "My own personal perspective on FBI agents is that as criminal investigators, they're great accountants. The actual reason they exist is to hoard computer data banks and show up briefly when it's time to make an arrest. Particularly if there are cameras. But I don't want you to share this sick perspective. So why am I telling you? I'm thinking out loud. Tired." She pressed her forefinger on the minute lines between her eyes. "Fucking suits. But hell, maybe Bender's having a good day. I think I'll call him. He tried to pat my rear once. Maybe there's a sentimental attachment."

Beth sat down, without being asked, and watched as Candy dialed the telephone.

"Bob!" Candy's voice was so genuinely jovial Beth couldn't believe her previous rancor had

121

been equally authentic. "Yeah . . . Oh, sure, well preserved, that's me." She paused. "No, actually, three guesses and I'll give you a bump on the first two . . . Bob, yes, you are a genius. The thing is, we have a sighting in Minnesota." Pause, during which Candy took the receiver from her ear and placed it against her forehead. "No, Bob, it feels just right. . . . How did you hear that? . . . Well, of course, we'll check it out first, but she could've walked in off the street, too, Bob. Shit, there's nothing that prevents old ladies from walking into hotel lobbies . . . Okay. . . . Okay. I'll call you back."

Candy buzzed her secretary and asked her to send Taylor to go over the Tremont guest lists again for unaccompanied senior citizens, women or men, and chat with the manager and the staff. As she talked, an anxious-looking intern brought in the mail. Candy began to slip through it absently, finally coming to an oversized bubble-lined book mailer stuffed nearly to bursting. Hanging up the telephone, she grinned at Beth.

"Another one," she said.

"You mean, stuff from a confessor?" They'd sent hand-drawn maps leading to nonexistent addresses and abandoned buildings where they said Ben was being held. They'd sent articles of brand-new clothing they said were Ben's. They'd sent photos of husbands they believed were responsible for the kidnapping, and — eeriest to Beth — long, rambling audio tapes in which they described how happy Ben was now that he was finally living in a Christian home. She suspected there were other tapes, sinister ones,

122

that Candy never shared.

Candy had told her early on that there were only three reasons someone would take a child: to get at that child's parent, economically or personally; to want a child and be crazy enough to think it was okay to take someone else's; or, in the very slimmest slice of a single percentage, to savage that child. Of the three, Candy told Beth, you hope for the crazy wanna-be parent, because that person will care for the child tenderly.

So the package could contain anything: a bloody T-shirt, a pair of already threadbare purple shorts, slashed and stiff with —

But Candy said, "No, I mean stuff from Rebecca, my former buddy in the academy, who is now a stockbroker." Using her thumbnail, Candy stripped open the mailer and shook out an astonishing pile of fuchsia and aqua garments — a tunic, elastic-waisted pants, a scarf, and a belt. "See, my buddy Rebecca gains and loses about thirty pounds every six months or so. It's a very expensive habit, because as soon as she starts getting fat, she starts mailing all her thin clothes to me." Candy shook her head. "The thing is, even when she looks good, Becks looks like the fortune-teller at a street fair. And so I end up taking these clothes to Saint Vincent De Paul — fortunately, Becks lives in California, so she never knows. And they probably cost hundreds of bucks."

Beth smiled. "Sounds like a muffled cry for help to me."

Candy held up the mailer. "Actually, it's a padded cry for help."

And Beth, to her horror, laughed, instantly covering her eyes and feeling that she was about to choke. Candy was on her feet and around the desk in seconds.

"Beth, Beth, listen," she said. "You laughed. You only laughed. If you laugh, it doesn't mean that's a point against our side. If you laugh, or read a book to Vincent, or eat something you like, it's not going to count for or against us on the big scoreboard of luck." Beth began to cry. "You have to believe me," Candy went on. "It feels like if you watch a movie, or listen to a song or do anything that makes you feel anything more than like absolute shit, that little moment of happiness is the thing that's going to be punished by losing Ben forever. But Beth, that's just not it. You're not going to kill your son because you laughed."

Humiliated even as she did it, Beth reached out and took Candy's hand, holding it against her cheek. Abruptly, Candy snatched it away, and Beth jumped up, nearly knocking over the chair.

"I didn't mean anything . . . " Beth said.

"I know, I know," Candy said. "I'm a jerk. There was absolutely nothing wrong with what you just did. I'm just an oversensitive jerk."

"You can't get involved," Beth said uncertainly.

"No," said Candy. "I mean, yes, to an extent. You can't get so involved you lose sight of things that could help people. But what that was about was . . . I'm a woman, I'm a detective supervisor, I'm Jewish. And I'm gay, did you know that? Every possible

124

kind of weirdness. So, I feel like the eyes of Texas are upon me, all the livelong day. I feel like every time I hug Katie Wright from Crimestoppers, somebody thinks I'm making a pass at her . . . "

"I wasn't trying — "

"I know you weren't. Jesus, I'm a jerk." Candy sat down. "But you know what? These bad clothes have given me a good idea. There's somebody I want us to go see, okay, Beth? You game?"

"Who?"

"There's this lady — the guys call her Crazy Mary; her name is actually Loretta Quail. Bad enough. Anyhow, what Loretta does is she helps people find stuff. Lost dogs. Lost money." She looked hard at Beth. "And sometimes, lost people." Once, Candy said, a young mother from Parkside drove off a bridge into a creek in the middle of a snowstorm. Her car went in head down and sank; the seat belt apparently malfunctioned. "She drowned in five feet of water, Beth. But the thing was, we didn't know. We didn't know what the hell had happened. This woman was going out for a bag of diapers. And she just never came back. The husband was a weasly little guy — we thought, you know, this woman's in the backyard under the play structure. They hadn't been having too good a time. But no, he was home the whole time with the baby — this lady was just gone. And so was her car. And none of her friends had seen her. She never got to the store. Just, you know, into the fourth dimension."

And so, Candy said, somebody mentioned Loretta. "You have to know, Beth, I'm a very kind of this-world person. So I thought, Well . . . you hear departments have pet psychics, but you never think . . . Anyhow, old Loretta sniffed this young mother's ski jacket just like those dogs Holmes and Watson, and said she was in her car under a mountain of snow, looking up. And Beth, that's just where she was. We found her the following March when the creek thawed, still in her seat belt, looking up at the roof of her car. The mountain of snow was what the village plowed off the street into the creek."

"So you think she might help find Ben."

"I think I'm going to offer this as an option to you, which I want you to keep under your hat. Except you can tell Pat, of course."

"I don't want to tell Pat."

"I think you should."

"Well, I don't want to tell Pat. When can we see her?"

"I'll call her now," said Candy; but the telephone rang, and Candy made a despairing motion that sent Beth out the door. As she watched through the glass, she got the impression Candy was arguing; her hands gave her away — she cradled the phone between her cheek and shoulder to gesture as if the caller could actually see her. She hung up and immediately made another short call.

Finally, looking spent, she came out and smiled. "Bender. He's decided as how he might mosey on over. Later," she said thinly. Beth, suddenly remembering the cannoli, handed over the box. Opening it, Candy said, "You keep doing this and I'm going to need Rebecca to mail me the *other* size." Grabbing a chunk off one end of the cannoli, she said, "Let's go see Loretta. She's home."

★ ★ ★

Loretta Quail's house was in what Beth's dad liked to call a 'changed neighborhood' — in other words, in Bill's opinion, a block that had long since lost the battle. Black middle schoolers, including one girl that Beth noticed to her shock was hugely pregnant, were playing pavement hockey in the street. Loretta's house looked like a threadbare fairyland in the midst of boarded windows and defeated lawns. From one end of the long hedge to the other, garishly painted ceramic elves disported themselves in various pursuits, from carving pumpkins to playing cards on a toadstool. When Loretta herself opened the door, a gust of trapped interior air, smelling of onions and spray starch, fastened itself to Beth's face like a wet washcloth. The inside of the house was as precious as the outside — every available surface was covered with china cats, carved wooden cats, stuffed cats, and not an insignificant number of the breathing variety. Beth counted six cats as Loretta took Candy's hand and led them inside, bustling back from her kitchen with a tray of mugs and a covered pot of tea. It must have been eighty degrees in the room, and Beth could see stray hairs clinging to the mug even at a distance; but she followed Candy's lead and bravely accepted herb tea and took one of the muffins that Loretta, to Beth's dismay, said she'd made herself.

"So, Loretta, you know we're here about Beth's son," Candy began.

"Oh, yes, of course," said Loretta. "And I knew you would come. But I thought it would be Friday. I had a dream last night that it was going to be Friday. I saw Beth in it." Dear God, thought Beth, madly glancing around the room at the hell of cats, she's nuts. Why do nuts women always have cats? Why not dogs, dogs who are just as excited to see you after you drive up to the corner to get milk as they were when they first met you, instead of cats, who, as Pat always said, regarded people as warm-blooded furniture? To keep her eyes to herself, Beth stared down at Loretta's ample thigh in its armor of polyester, a blue that did not exist in nature. Why did nuts women aged about sixty-five who kept cats also wear stretch pants? With flowered blouses that looked chosen carefully for their potential to make the wearer look like ten miles of bad road under a tablecloth? Because something like these clothes had looked good on them when they were young? Because everything else looked worse? As she let her glance slide upward to Loretta's tightly furled perm, like a head full of late-spring buds, she heard the woman ask Candy, "So, do you want me to do a trance? Or just give you some impressions?"

Beth thought, How about a side of slaw with

128

that? She felt wildly, hideously embarrassed. Not ever in her life — not once, even the single time she'd dropped acid as a college senior — had Beth ever had an experience she considered truly extrasensory. Hunches, feelings, semiprayers overlaid with coincidences — those, yes; her family of origin ran on those things, as if superstition were gasoline. But though the inside of her brain was lined with her grandmother Kerry's tales of dead aunts whose spirits jetted to Chicago without benefit of airplanes to warn that Katie or Mary from Louisiana had died in the flu epidemic, Beth herself had never smelled Evie's cologne, or felt her mother's spirit brush past her, even though several intelligent friends who had lost parents had assured Beth that these things would happen to her.

So when Loretta began explaining the origin of her gift, how smells had begun 'throwing' her into trances when she was six, Beth had to struggle with muscles jumping in her face. It was impolite, but on reflection Beth realized that Loretta was probably used to clients who behaved oddly. She didn't seem bothered when Beth put her hand over her eyes as if the light were too bright. Sounding as though she were reciting from a script, she explained to Beth that the first time it happened was after she'd survived an attack of measles, and that in the trances "it was always the same thing — I'd see things in the funniest places. Things I couldn't explain. They weren't mine. A wallet under the wheel of a wagon. A man in a bus station, trying to hide his face behind a bandanna. A ring in the vent of a clothes dryer. And after a couple of years of these things going on about twice a month, I started to tell my mama, and my mama started to tell her friends, and it turned out that every single one of these things was lost. The people, too. And when I remembered every single one of the pictures — I used to call them 'my pictures' — I'd seen, well, God in heaven, people found all kinds of things."

"Are you ever wrong?" asked Candy.

"I've never been wrong," said Loretta.

"Never?"

"There have been times when people haven't found the things they were missing. I can't always say, 'This jewelry, or this document, is in a file cabinet in the basement of a house on Addison Street.' I can't give everybody an address. There have been times when I haven't been able to trance, usually because the people who had lost the things didn't really want to find them. You know, like a teenage girl might be a prostitute. That happens a lot. But every time I do see something, I really see it. It's where I see it. I know that. Most of your psychics average about fifty percent; and the ones in the magazines and the newspapers, I don't think even twenty percent of the things they say will come to pass ever does. They're just good public relations people is all. Most of them will tell you this is a gift from God, even while they've got their hands out for the gimme. Well, I believe in the Lord, but I don't think this is a gift from God; I think it's a wiring problem in my head. I've helped out more than five hundred people. But I've got this idea I shouldn't trade on it. I've never taken a nickel for it and I never will. I've never talked to the press and I never will." She glanced ironically around her tiny living room. "If I had, I'd be living at One Michigan Boulevard instead of here. I've found some . . . pretty valuable things."

She held out her hand for Ben's shoe, which Candy slid from its sealed plastic evidence bag, put her nose inside the heel of the shoe, and inhaled deeply. She grinned at Beth. "New shoes," she said. "But you can definitely tell he's in there. Yes indeed."

Loretta took another bite from her muffin, turning the shoe one way and then another in her large hand. Then, all at once, she dropped the muffin. Beth yipped. The big woman lolled back in her chair; her mouth dropped open and a line of saliva slid slowly down the crease between her lip and the edge of her jaw. Beth stared at Candy, who held up her hand warningly. Just as abruptly, Loretta sat up and dusted the crumbs from her legs.

"Well," she said. "This is a funny one. I saw the little boy, but I only saw him for a second. Saw *him*, that is. The rest of the time, I saw what he was thinking. That's only happened to me about twice before in my life."

"What was he thinking?" Candy whispered, slowly, hunching forward in her chair.

"Well, he wasn't so much thinking . . . it was, he was dreaming. Yes, that's absolutely it. Dreaming. Asleep. He was in a polished wooden box. He was lying on some soft lacy

131

material. The box had a big lid that was shut over him, curved . . . "

"He was dreaming he was in this box?" Candy urged her.

"In this . . . kind of box. Longer than he's tall . . . "

There was nothing else it could be, nothing. Beth didn't want to scream. She tried to hold her mouth closed with both her cupped hands, but she opened her mouth anyway and screamed, "I knew it!" Her knuckles against her front teeth began to bleed.

"Beth, wait! Hear her out!" Candy tried to keep Beth on her chair, but Beth was up, trying to shake Candy off. All the cats in the room stood up, hissing.

Mildly, Loretta turned to Candy, shaking her head. "Sometimes, this is what happens when you tell them. They don't want to hear. Do you want me to stop?"

7

"I DON'T don't know why cognac," said Candy, shoving the snifter at Beth as she sat down at the table in the first chain fern restaurant they came across. Candy had squealed into the parking lot as if the motor were on fire. "Maybe because in the movies, they always give you a shot of brandy if you have a shock. Works for me."

Candy sat down across from Beth at the sticky four-top, "I want to eat something. You want to eat something?" The more time she spent with Candy, the clearer it became to Beth that Candy ate enormous amounts of food, always, and never looked anything but concave; perhaps, Beth thought idly now, she was bulimic. As Beth shook her head, dismissing food, experimentally sipping the cognac, Candy told a waitress, "I'll have a . . . smoked chicken pizza, with double cheese and . . . shrimp too." Leaning over, she told Beth, "If my mother were dead, she'd be rolling in her grave."

"Why?" Beth asked.

"Because the cheese and the meat and the shrimp — this is probably the most trayf thing you could eat." She grinned at Beth's bewildered look. "You know, not kosher. My mother had a kosher kitchen. But I got to be eighteen, you know, I grew up in Florida, for God's sake. And I thought, If you're not going to eat lobster, why live? Anyway, that's just the smallest part of why the Jewishness never caught on — religiously, that is."

"It never seemed like much of a religion for women," Beth ventured.

"Not like Catholicism, huh?"

"No, I didn't mean that. It's just as bad. But I don't really do Catholicism. I told you that."

"But at least you don't have to immerse yourself in scummy water once a month so you'll be clean enough to sleep with your sacred husband."

"Did you ever do that?"

"I told you, Beth. I don't have a husband, right?"

"Sure, right."

"But of course, if I did, I wouldn't. That's the real dark side of religious belief. You might as well handle snakes or something. Drink some more of your brandy."

Beth drank. She could picture the beaker of her stomach being coated, the outline of it glowing red, maybe purple.

"Do you feel better now?" Candy asked. "Because I want to tell you something."

"You can tell me."

"I don't think what Loretta meant was what you thought she meant."

"It was obvious."

"No, she never said that. After you were out in the car, she repeated to me that if she didn't *say* the child was dead, she didn't *mean* the child was dead. She would have said that."

"You heard her. You heard what she said

134

about the curved wooden box."

"Well, Loretta can't account for what she sees in trance, Beth. She says that all the time; people have to tell *her* what stuff means. That box could have been anything. A symbol of some kind. I mean, this woman has a little light in the piazza. We can't know for sure what she meant, but when I go back and talk to her — I'm not taking you — I'm going to ask her for more to go on. More impressions. I just don't want you to give up because of what some loony said. I mean, Loretta is a very nice loony, but really, Beth, we have no proof that anything at all has happened to Ben."

Candy ordered Beth another drink and went on. "I shouldn't have brought you there."

Beth said, "I wanted to." Candy eating her pizza was like a fire ant, tiny, delicate, and absolutely voracious. She whacked the pizza into six neat slices and nibbled each methodically to the crust. "Don't you eat your crust?" Beth asked, embarrassed by her motherly tone.

"My mother told me it would make my hair curly," said Candy. "So, of course, I wanted my hair just exactly the opposite way."

"You look like Gloria Steinem," Beth said, wondering if she was getting drunk.

"So says everyone," Candy replied, polishing off the pizza, ordering herself a vodka and tonic. She looked up sharply. "I'm not on duty, Beth. I just want you to know. I wouldn't have a drink if I was on duty. I mean, I'm not on duty any more than I'm ever not on duty. I come in on almost all my days off."

"Why?"

"Very tedious personal life."

"Come on."

"No, I really do have not much of a life. It's not uncommon for female cops."

"Why?"

"Well, this life, this work, it's hard enough for a guy who has a wife and the wife runs the house and stuff to have a normal life. But for a woman, who doesn't have a wife at home, it's almost impossible. You can just do so many things. I mean, if I join the book club, I'm going to make it to one meeting a year, and at that meeting my beeper's going to go off."

"Don't you go on vacation?"

"Once a year, up north in Wisconsin, with my sister's family. And a few days in spring to see my mother in Florida when she's there."

"And don't you have a . . . partner?"

"Not now." Candy brushed her forehead.

Beth didn't know what to say next. Was she being too personal? What the hell, Beth thought.

"Is there a lot of — " Beth paused, gulped, and went on — "a lot of prejudice against you on the department?"

"Not as much as in my own family," said Candy, smiling broadly, her even teeth so perfect Beth wondered, Can they be real? "No, not anymore. You can't be overt about that stuff much anymore. But when I was a kid, and I started, you had to be really sure nobody ever knew. I mean *nobody*."

"Not even your . . . chief guy?"

"Especially not brass. Because you couldn't get hired on a department if you were what they called then a 'deviate'. They would do these background checks on you, talk to your family . . . they still do this stuff if you're going to be . . ."

"What?" Beth asked, speaking carefully now, aware that she would slur if she didn't enunciate. "A spy?"

"No, even if you're going to be in the FBI, I think. Certainly, politicians and judges and stuff."

Candy then described her rookie-cop self, a twenty-five-year-old self, as resembling, for want of a better comparison, James Dean. Beth, increasingly sleepy, tried to imagine dainty, long-legged Candy in leather biker boots tucked into jeans, with her long, soft, straight hair ear-length and slicked back from her forehead. "It's hard to picture," she said.

"For me, too." Candy laughed. "I always liked pretty clothes. I was on homecoming court, high school and college. You ask my mother, she'll say that my desperado period was my first attempt to kill her." Candy combed her hair with four fingers. "But I think it was, I'd figured out I was gay and I thought there was one way you had to look. That you had to look like a man." It was in a gay bar, she said, that someone had passed Candy, who was then working as a research assistant for a lawyer, a want ad for Tampa city 'police matrons', and dared her to apply. "That's what we were then. We couldn't go to the academy. We couldn't work with anything but juveniles. That was the standard." She applied, and got the job largely because of the glowing recommendations of her neighbor, a nearsighted old woman who had her confused with the sweet-faced teacher at a Christian preschool who lived across the hall. "She's a wonderful girl," Candy recalled the neighbor telling the officer who came to check out applicant Bliss. "Very quiet and religious."

And who could doubt a sweet little old lady? "They regretted it, though," sighed Candy. "Because after a couple of years, I started noticing guys I'd trained advancing through ranks, getting paid twice what I was, and I sued, and I won . . . I won my gun."

"You didn't have guns?"

"The chief used to say, 'I don't want my female officers to be killers.' Jesus." Candy shook her head. "Now they pick the daintiest little cutie-pie things they can find to go undercover with the drug wolves. They play better."

"Are those cutie pies gay, too?"

Candy motioned for another drink, and as she did, her eyes narrowed and locked on a space just over Beth's shoulder. But she tried to go on as if she weren't staring. Did Beth dare turn her head, follow Candy's eyes? "Uh, no," Candy said. "Not all. There are plenty of female officers who are straight now, not that there are plenty of female officers, I mean . . . Beth, will you excuse me a moment?"

Beth did turn then. She didn't recognize the officer, who wore a state trooper's ample felt hat and kept his arms folded in front of him the entire time he talked to Candy, towering over her, looking down at her as if she were a child. Only his head moved, gesturing repeatedly to the right, as if he were pointing outside the window to his sleek black-and-silver squad. Candy looked back at the table, and Beth thought instantly, She's sober. She's sober, and that means this has to do with something big, awful, with me. She felt the crotch of her jeans dampen minutely as her bladder, never strong since Kerry, began to let go — got up and rushed for the washroom, where she cursorily threw up the brandy, scrubbed her tongue and her face with soap and paper towels, and combed her hair.

When she came out, Candy was standing in the foyer with Beth's purse over one shoulder and her own over the other. The table had been cleared; the state trooper was standing outside, next to his car. Crossing the room, Beth thought, would not be possible. Would the other diners notice if she got down on all fours and began to crawl? She was sure she could make it then, with the stability of four limbs and the nearness of firm ground. She took one step, wavered, and Candy came striding over to her and took hold with a vise-clamp grip under Beth's armpit. They walked out into the parking lot, dazzled with the late-afternoon sun.

"Beth," said Candy, "you're right. I know you're scared, but this isn't necessarily anything either. We have to know, that's all. We have to know."

"What?" Beth gasped. "What?"

"We . . . that is . . . they have found a body,"
Candy said. "It is a child, and it is a boy. But
that's all we know, Beth. That's absolutely all
we know."

"Where?"

"Well, the body was found by birdwatchers
in Saint Michael's Reservoir — that's near
Barrington, you know? North of here, maybe
an hour. It's been there some time, maybe
much too long for it to be Ben. But we have
to know."

"I meant, where is he? Where is he now?"

"Beth, I am going to drive you to your in-laws'
house, and then we will decide who will go to
the county with me to do an identification. It
does not have to be you. It does not have to
be Pat. It does have to be someone who could
make a reasonably certain identification of Ben
if Ben had died. Someone who knows Ben very
well."

"I'll go."

"No, I think — " Candy opened the door of
her car and absently ducked the back of Beth's
neck with the heel of her palm, as if Beth were
handcuffed and liable to hit her head on the side
of the car — "I think we'll just get to Angelo's
and then we'll decide on this. No one is going
anywhere. I mean, we have time." Candy slipped
the buckle of Beth's seat belt into the notch and
locked it.

"Is he dead?" God, thought Beth, how she is
looking at me! "No, I mean, I know he's dead,
but *how* did he die? Was he murdered? Did he
drown?"

140

"There hasn't been any time to determine what the cause of death was, Beth," said Candy. "The body was only found a couple of hours ago, and the state guys did the match from our bulletin, and the child will be taken by ambulance to the county about the same time as . . ."

They pulled into Angelo's driveway, which was thronged with photographers and print reporters, who for once seemed to have outflanked the TV people; it was, after all, a long time until the ten o'clock news. But a Channel Two truck screeched into the driveway before Candy could even open her door, blocking her. She was out and crouched like a prizefighter before Beth could move. The reporter's feet hit the pavement at the same moment.

"Move your car," Candy said quietly.

"Chief," pleaded the reporter, a blond man in his early thirties, "is it true? Did they find Ben Cappadora's body?"

"Move your fucking car," said Candy, not raising her voice. "You are obstructing a police vehicle."

"Just wait one minute — "

"Taylor," called Candy, and Calvin Taylor came loping down from Angelo and Rosie's porch. "Can you please arrest this man for obstruction while I get Beth in to her family?" Taylor made as if to reach into his back pocket, and the young reporter turned and fled, the truck backing out of the drive directly into the path of another of its species. Candy rushed Beth up the front stoop, while reporters called, softly,

141

as if from a great distance, "Have you seen the body, Beth? Is it Ben? Are you okay, Beth?"

A reporter on the porch stepped in front of Candy as she shoved open the door. "I'm from the *New York Times*," he said with well-bred earnestness.

"Good career move," said Candy, closing the door behind her.

Beth was reminded of a child's picture book, in which a ring of widemouthed frog brothers and sisters gathered each night around the edge of the bog to hear their mother tell a story. Angelo and Rosie, old-people fashion, had their three sofas arranged end-to-end against three walls — no fancy conversation nooks and parlor tables at odd angles for them. And on all three sofas were arranged the silent cast of main characters, at least those who could be assembled so quickly: Ellen, Pat, Monica, Joey and Tree, Pat's parents, Barbara Kelliher. Pat got up immediately and enfolded Beth in a hard hug; she could smell his sweat — a wild, high animal odor unlike anything she'd ever smelled on her husband's body. No one else moved. The two phone lines in the house, the police line and the family's, rang incessantly, though Beth could hear officers, more than a few, talking in the kitchen. As Pat held her, Beth's father and her brother Bick burst through the back door; Beth heard her father say, "Jesus bleeding Christ, these vampires, these vampires! Where's Bethie?" She ran from Pat's arms into her brother's; Bick was big, and she could lean on him without feeling she was going to have to bear the weight.

"Is it true, Bethie?" he asked. "Is it Ben?"

"I don't know, I don't know," she said into his sport coat lapel, finally, blessedly, able to cry.

"Folks, listen now," Candy said. "We would ordinarily try to do some fingerprint analysis here first. But in this situation, this body has been exposed to . . . wildlife elements, and there is damage to the extremities. So Ben's fingerprint record is not going to do us much good. What we can do is wait for the forensic dentist . . . this shouldn't take more than a couple of hours to get — "

"No," said Bick hoarsely. "We want to know if it's Ben."

Candy pressed her finger to the spot between her eyes. "Of course you do, of course you do — okay, okay." She motioned to several officers who stood just inside the back door. "McGuire, Elliott, I'm going to drive Beth and Pat. Taylor and those three from state will stay here with the rest of the family; you two drive whoever else wants to come, or we can get the other guy — what's his name? — Buckman — to drive somebody. Okay?"

"I am not going," said Angelo suddenly, the first to speak. He's old, thought Beth, dumbfounded, as if seeing her father-in-law again after many years. He's an old man.

"I think I should stay here with Rosie and Angelo," Bill offered slowly, as his son cast him a glance of pure spite.

143

"It's okay," Beth told Bick. "Don't worry. So long as you go."

"I'll identify the body," Bick said, holding Beth harder.

"Mr. Kerry," Candy asked him gently, "are you sure, first of all, sure you want to go through this, and secondly, sure that you know the child well enough . . . ?"

"Ben is my nephew. He's named after me. I've known Ben since the day he was born."

"But have you seen him often enough recently . . . ?"

"God damn it to hell!" Bick shouted, startling Beth. "I see my nephew all the time!"

"I'll do it," Pat whispered.

"Paddy, no," Beth told him. "No. You can't."

"He's my baby."

"No, you can't and I can't."

"Okay, let's go," Candy instructed, and the officers formed a phalanx of broad shoulders around them, shoulders in blue cotton and corduroy, military in their resolve. Candy opened the door. Ellen held one of Beth's hands, Pat the other. The cars were lined up nose-to-tail in the driveway. "No news, no news," Candy called briskly to the now-teeming crowd on the lawn; Angelo's June roses were a mire of mud and trampled blooms. "Let the family pass by now."

As the officers threw open the doors, Beth drew back. "I don't want to ride with Pat," she said suddenly. Pat stared at her. "I mean, I don't care if he rides, too, but I want my

144

brother," What, she thought, what's wrong with your goofy face, Pat? "I have to tell him something," she finished, gesturing stupidly, fingers to mouth. Pat turned away. Then there was the airtight swish of the instantly locking squad-car doors. The reporters ran for their cars and vans, but they didn't dare go as fast as Candy did when she slapped on her portable Mars light and hit the expressway, a hundred miles an hour, talking quietly to the officer beside her the whole time as if they were driving five miles an hour in a parade.

Beth had stood outside a great many morgue doors, some at hospitals, some at prisons, some at disaster sites, photographing stretchers with their cased black-plastic burdens. But she'd never been inside one. It looked like a school corridor, with frosted glass windows in blond doors. Candy led the marching V of officers surrounding them to an elevator. "This is what Cook County defines as a waiting room," she said, pointing to a shaky collection of green leather sofas and chairs, some gouting stuffing. "I'm going to take Bick upstairs. What he is going to see is a view of the child's face and pertinent . . . well, through glass. If he has any questions, we'll come back for Ellen. Or someone."

This, thought Beth, was not like the hospital. There were no heroic medical gymnastics taking place out of sight in noisy, isolated, sterile rooms overhead, no frantic last measures to preserve a life, just so everyone could believe that every stop had been pulled out, every last hope, however futile, exercised. She remembered the atmosphere of bustle outside her mother's door in intensive care; legions of nurses and caissons of equipment rumbled in and out at the speed of light. Here, people Beth assumed were doctors, perhaps even medical examiners, strolled, perusing clipboards; technicians carrying trays of tubing moved briskly but not frantically. Pat leaned against the wall, under a sign that pictured a burning cigarette enclosed in a red-slashed circle, and smoked; Beth noticed the floor was, in fact, littered with butts.

"It's all over here," she said, not realizing until Ellen looked at her that she'd actually spoken.

"We don't know that, Beth, There is every reason to believe Ben is still alive," Ellen replied firmly, in her very best Ellen voice, the voice that said there was a better than fifty-fifty chance that Nick would come back to her in senior year after he'd fallen in love with the Swedish girl at drama camp. And he had. The voice that had told her, when Kerry didn't move inside Beth for a full week, that babies near full term sometimes hardly moved at all, that it was perfectly normal. And it was.

"No there isn't," Beth said pettishly, wanting to tell Ellen all about the psychic, wanting to tell Pat — had that been just a few hours ago? Had nobody told Pat about Loretta? Where had Pat been anyway? Beth realized with a shock that she hadn't seen Vincent or Kerry at all — who had her children? Who cared? "No," she told Ellen again. "There's not every reason to believe that."

146

She breathed in slowly. "Anyway, it's probably better if he isn't — "

"Oh Christ, Bethie, be quiet now — you're talking out of your mind," said Joey, and Pat lit another cigarette.

The elevator doors sighed open. It was Candy. Everyone strained forward. She held up both elegant hands. "They're getting the procedure ready now. Bick's fine. I just wanted you to know that this is going to take a little while. Hang on. I'm going to come down here with him as soon as I possibly can. Okay, Beth? Okay, Pat?"

Everyone slumped back against the green leather seats. There was to be a wait, then. Beth felt like a hostess, like she should be offering everyone something to drink. No one spoke — a minute by the huge clock on the wall. What would a regular woman say? Beth asked herself. A regular woman would ask about her children. "Ellenie," she began carefully, "who's taking care of — ?"

She did not get to finish, because Bick came lurching out of the stairwell, his arm over his eyes, the click of Candy's heels close behind him, and then she, too, out the door. Wait, Beth thought — we were supposed to get a wait. "Wait!" she said aloud, as Bick fell down on the sofa next to her, hunched over, tears pouring.

"Bethie, Bethie, it's not Ben," he said.

"Uh . . . wait," Beth said again, trying to lift one of her arms, her impossibly waterlogged and heavy arms.

"Are you sure?" Pat was on his knees in front

147

of Bick, searching his face.

"He's way too small, and his hair, it's red hair, but it's like strawberry blond. He's really a baby, Bethie — oh, he's somebody's baby, Bethie. His little face was like he was asleep — he wasn't even wrecked, not his face — oh, Bethie, it's not Ben."

"Oh, thank you, God," Pat breathed. "It's not him, it's not him! It's not Ben." Pat stopped, looking hard at Beth. "Beth, aren't you glad?"

Beth said, "Glad?"

8

THE house was what she had been dreading, thought Beth, the house after all. When Pat turned off the engine and got out of the car, he did not seem to notice that Beth didn't get up, even when Kerry, vigorously using one of her lexicon of four words, began wailing, "Out, out, out!"

To Pat's back, Beth said, "It wasn't you. It was the house."

Pat ignored her; he rarely responded to what Beth said anymore. And that was just as well — half of what Beth said made no sense even to her, at least out of context.

"You were hurt because I stayed in Chicago all summer. You kept saying I should come home, and I kept saying I couldn't," Beth tried again. "But now I know why, honey. It wasn't because I thought I would really find Ben. And it wasn't that I didn't want to be with you. It was really that I didn't want to go into my house. See?"

Pat had already gone inside. She was alone in the garage, literally talking to the dashboard as the automatic light winked out overhead and the door slid shut behind her, severing the reach of the pale afternoon sun. Pat had taken the baby out of her car seat and gone inside. I'm cold, Beth thought suddenly. She resisted the urge to hug herself warm and sat in the dark car with her arms neatly aligned along her sides. I'm cold, because it's a cold day in August. You got them in Wisconsin, even in the baked-hard center of a string of droughty days, a single day of surprise chill that wagged a warning finger under your nose of the season to come.

Fall. A brand-new page. The time that for most of her life felt to Beth like the real beginning of the year, perhaps because the resumption of school seemed to signal a toughening of expectations. That summer, as one hot vivid day slid through a sweaty night into another, Beth had stopped wondering where she was when she awoke, heart racing, alone in Rosie's guest room. It was as if she had never had a home or a job or a family. She had been born to the routine — out of Rosie's icy house into the breathtaking blast of the driveway, the murmur of the reporters (whose names she knew by now, who maintained a kind of beach-party atmosphere on the lawn even though no one, not one of the family, not one of the volunteers, ever gave them an interview), into the Find Ben center, the round of paper-folding and stamping people gave her to do, until, after an hour or so, she felt fretful. Out into the heat again, bum a Camel from Joey at the catering company, past a handful of reporters in the lobby of the Parkside station, up past the Cappadora command center in the second-floor conference room (everyone waved), up the short flight, turn, into Candy's office.

Candy. Why, Beth wondered then and later, did Candy let her sit there for hours, watching her talk on the phone, listening to her conversations with other officers, her instructions, her interviews, even, occasionally, her rebukes of subordinates, her tense interchanges with the chief or the president of the village board? Probably, Candy had understood from the first that Beth was unable to really take in and record substance, to digest or collate the intricate overlapping webs of the investigation and its politics. Candy let Beth sit in her office, Beth felt, rather like you might indulge an old dog with the kind of worshipful eyes that made you forget how capable he was of fouling the carpet. Only there, under the protection of Candy's delicate efficiency, did she feel elementally linked to Ben, or even elementally alive.

The rest of the time, there were roles, all with certain motions to perform: brave, obedient daughter-in-law; grieving mother; plucky friend; loyal wife. She could do them, however awkwardly. But the motions were themselves exhausting in their ultimate uselessness. Like brute and repetitive muscle exercise, they ate time and kept Beth in shape for . . . for what? For the resumption of a life, an altered life, post-Ben, which Beth couldn't really imagine, but which she figured might sometime be expected of her. What she did know was that some sort of reckoning, some sort of relinquishment, would precede stepping up onto the verge of that life. And though she didn't know when the step would have to be taken, she did not want to take it without Candy beside her. If she did, oh, it would be worse than dying, worse then remembering the day Ben had called her 'my beauteous grape' — the day she had come to believe that Ben was not just good and lovely but stuffed with poetry — worse than the photocopied stories she sometimes got hold of in the center before anyone thought to stop her, stories about sexually tortured babies kept alive for months, photographed in their agonies. Beth was afraid that she might kill people, or masturbate outside, or drive Angelo's Lincoln Town Car through a crowded preschool playground. So she did all the good girl things, and hoarded her real consciousness for Candy's office, for the few moments of the hour or many hours she spent there each day when she could drop all her masks.

For Candy, there was evidently no such thing as too bluntly. She did not look away when Beth said she hoped Ben was dead, not because she could ever stop missing him but because then at least she could know that he had stopped missing her. When she said Vincent and Kerry would be better off without her, Candy didn't disagree; she simply reminded Beth that she had to play the hand she was dealt. Two weeks after the body of the baby who was not Ben was found, Beth read in the *Tribune* that the odds of finding a child decreased geometrically after the first week. And Candy had simply told her that this was true, but to ignore it, because that the first thing a cop learned was that there were lies, damned lies, and statistics.

Candy further pointed out that the child

who'd been found in the reservoir, finally identified as two-year-old Chad Sweet of Glen Ellyn, missing for four months, had not been kidnapped. He'd drowned accidentally when his seventeen-year-old father took him fishing without a life preserver. The terrified kid had been afraid to tell anyone but his equally terrified eighteen-year-old girlfriend, the baby's mother. So, while Candy did try to give Beth a hopeful spin on the facts where possible, she did not tell Beth to keep making novenas for a miracle, as Tree did. She did not keep bugging her to let just one big, national magazine do an eight-page spread, the way Laurie did ("Why not spread the goddamn net wider, so that the just-one-person who needs to see Ben's face will? Why not, Beth?").

Most of all, Candy did not tell Beth to go home. Everyone else — Rosie, Ellen, even Bick and Paul, whose love Beth counted as primal — had made this a litany. Candy had waited for Beth to feel ready to talk about going home.

That happened one evening when Beth was hanging around Candy's office late, and Candy had seemed to notice Beth afresh as she stood up around seven to turn out her office light.

"Do you want to go get some dinner?" Candy asked.

They took hot dogs from Mickey's and drove all the way down to the Lincoln Park lagoons, out to the grassy edge of the ponds, while a dozen or so black boys, each sleeker and more beautiful than the one before, threw handfuls of illegal fireworks across the water at one another.

The air around them throbbed with old Motown tunes from the open windows of their cars. Beth hesitated when the boys looked their way, at what must have seemed two old and impossibly crazy white women picking their way through the hot night.

"Don't worry," Candy said. "I have a gun." At Beth's look, she laughed. "For Christ's sake, Beth. They're only kids throwing firecrackers. Not that I don't mean it. If they start to kill each other or us, I'll shoot them." They sat down on the dry grass.

Beth said, then, "Everyone thinks I should go home."

"What do *you* think?" Candy asked, halfway through her own bag of fries and already eyeballing Beth's. Beth nudged it toward her.

"I think they have a point. I don't want to, though."

"Do you think if you leave, we won't find Ben?"

"Maybe. I don't think you'll find Ben anyhow, not really. I just don't . . . " Beth leaned back and lay on the grass — how impossibly winsome and sweet, a starry summer night, the kind of night that once invited something, a clean two-mile run, lovemaking, rocking a baby on the porch. "I don't think I can go back and start up life as if none of this ever happened."

"Do you think anyone expects you to do that?"

"I don't mean just Ben missing. I mean, as if there was never any Ben."

"Do you think anyone — ?"

154

"No. No, nobody expects me to go on like that. Except maybe *I* expect me to do that. Because I think it's the only way I can go on at all."

"I know that when people lose a child or anyone significant in their lives, they often find it helpful to get some counseling."

"Detective Supervisor Bliss, you sound so professional."

"Come on. There are groups, Beth, grief groups. They do really good work — I mean *really* good work."

"If I go to one of those things, that means it's all over."

"No, it doesn't. It means that a part of it is beginning. The part where you try to take stock of what you can do and how you can do it. You have to survive, Beth."

"That's it. That's just it. I don't want to survive Ben. I don't want to try to outrun him — it — this. I don't want to survive it and I don't want to face it."

"So you stay here and live in the corner of my office. Which I don't mind. But I'm going to have to start hanging my coat on you eventually."

"I should go home."

"Beth, you do whatever you need to do. But however lousy a mother you feel like right now, you are the only mother Kerry and Vincent have."

"What a bargain."

"I think they could do a whole lot worse."

"Oh, I don't."

"I do. And if you go home, Beth, it doesn't mean that . . . " Beth looked up from the ground into Candy's dove-colored eyes, which were always all-iris, eyes that looked made for a camera. "It's not a trade, Beth. I've told you this. If you give everything else up, it doesn't mean you get Ben. If that was the way it worked, I'd tell you to do it."

"I know."

"You have these two great kids, Bethie. I would give my right arm to have a kid like Kerry."

"People do it. People . . . like you do it all the time."

"No, not people like me. Gay women, yes. But not people like me. I mean, I could. But Beth, you don't become a cop because you're a rebel. I'm a deeply conventional person, Beth. I know that sounds crazy, given my . . . well, just leave it at that. I always thought I'd have a husband and kids. I just couldn't ever see the husband."

"But you could . . . "

"No. Sometimes I think . . . " Candy paused to stuff her mouth with a fistful of fries. "There's this guy. We're old buddies. He was my law professor — I went to a year of law school, during my Watergate period. He had a crush on me, a bad crush, and I had to tell him I didn't do men, that is, not anymore. Which is to say, I have, in my life, though I can't imagine why I'm telling you that. Jesus. Anyhow, Chris and I, we hang out. We get Chinese, maybe once a month. Watch Spencer Tracy movies.

He's probably, Chris is probably forty-seven
or something now. And he's this perennial
bachelor. Dates young women. Coeds. I have
sweaters older. And then, of course, me. We
go to the ballet and stuff. To his big firm gala
things. I tell him, Chris, I'm your beard — you
know what that means, Beth?" Beth nodded; she
didn't. "I'm like his surrogate wife for places he
can't take the young chickies."

Candy lay back on her elbows, Beth wincing
over the contact of the grass with the fine beige
linen. "A few Christmases ago, I had this party
— I told you I'm a bad Jew — and he brought
this girl. Beth, I don't think she could drive
yet. And I told him, 'Chris, you're going to be
hanging around the middle school soon. This is
getting fairly despicable.' And he looked at me
so sadly. I thought, I had this flash, he's gay, or
he's something, and he's not out to himself. Not
at all. But what he said was, 'I'm tired, Candy.
I want a son. I would marry you, Candy. You
name the day.'"

Candy went on, "And since that Christmas,
I've thought about it. I've thought, why not?
We have a lot of laughs. He's still looking at
the teenagers, but they aren't looking back that
much anymore. With what I make, if I had a
kid, I'd have to chain it to the bed while I'm
at work; and my work is crazy. But if I had
enough money to cover it all . . . Chris is richer
than God. I mean, why not? He'd have his kid
. . . I'd have a kid."

"But you'd be betraying . . . who you are."

Candy smiled slowly. "Don't we all do that,

157

Beth? Shit, can you please point out why I am telling you all this?"

The teenagers were drifting back to their cars. The air smelled of cordite from the last wisps of firework smoke.

"I don't mind," Beth said, thinking, That was lame. "I'm glad you did."

"I guess I am because this is horrible, what's happening to you, Beth. It's the worst, the absolute shits. But it doesn't mean you should throw away everything else with both hands."

She doesn't see, thought Beth sadly. Not even Candy. She doesn't see that if I can't be Ben's mother, I not only don't want to be anyone's mother, I don't want to be anyone. Even being dead would be an effort. I want to be a lay sister, scrubbing the same patch of stone cement floor every day, scrubbing, scrubbing.

"And one more thing," Candy said, wadding up the paper wrappings. "If you go home, it doesn't mean I'll forget you or stop working to find Ben. I'll work every day, Bethie. As long as it takes. And if you want to call me every day and make sure I'm working, you can. And I'll call you, too. All the time. I promise."

★ ★ ★

So three weeks later, Pat came with the baby on Saturday night. And Beth told him she would be going home on Sunday. Pat's face reflected comic-book disbelief, dropped jaw and all. There was a hushed sort of festivity in the house afterward; she could hear Joey and Tree

158

hanging around to sit up late in the kitchen with Angelo — even the reporters seemed restless. As if it were part of the choreography, Beth let Pat make love to her for the first time since the reunion; he'd brought her diaphragm to her, unasked, several weeks before, in mute appeal. She had taken the box in her hand and laughed, right into his crumpling face. But then he had done the most touching thing, a thing Beth realized objectively she had not sufficient grace to do. He had turned back to her and asked, "Why don't you want to? I mean, it isn't really the actual sex I want. It's you. It's your love."

"I love you, Pat," she had said. "It's just that making love would be something so . . . ordinary, so . . . "

"Normal?"

"I guess."

"Do we have to never do anything normal again, Bethie? Is that what we have to do for Ben?"

"I don't know if I ever can. Do anything the way I would have done it . . . before."

"I don't know if I ever can either, Beth. I know that I'm lonely, though. I feel like I didn't just lose my kid but my wife, too. Like I'm a widower, and I don't want to be."

I do, Beth thought, but she said, "Let me take a little time."

And when it finally happened, it wasn't so bad. Beth had not even been able to imagine that her body would open for Pat; but it turned out to be an accommodating body, after all; and though she felt as though her insides were covered with skin, as though Pat's shudderings and urgings were calisthenic rather than romantic, the tenderness she experienced for him, though at a distance at least equal to the width of the room, when he finally rolled over beside her, cupping one of her breasts gratefully in his hand as he fell asleep, made it a good thing to have done. Pat whistled in the morning as they packed the car.

Just before they left, when Angelo and Rosie and the girls were lined up on the curb, Ellen's Saab screeched to a halt behind them. She had David in his Sunday-school clothes on the seat beside her. Beth jumped out of the front seat to hug her.

"I thought you were going to leave without saying goodbye," Ellen told her, instantly beginning to cry.

"I called you."

"I was on the way."

"It's the right thing."

"I'll be back next weekend."

"And I'm going to keep everything going . . . "

"I know, Ellenie. You're the top, you're the best."

They hugged, but Beth felt the slackening, the dip. The principals were leaving; who could expect the supporting actors to go on with the show alone?

"It's all my fault," Ellen said suddenly.

"What?"

"I put your room on my card, so you had to go up to the desk and take so long getting it straightened out . . . "

"Ellenie," Beth said, trying to be gentle. "I would have had to go up to the desk anyway . . . "

And yet, how many times had she thought exactly the same thing?

"I even talked you into coming, remember? You said you were still too fat from Kerry. I made you come."

"You didn't."

"I made you come. I signed you up without even asking you, Beth, remember?"

"It doesn't matter, Ellen. It just happened. It just happened."

Pat got out of the car and put his arm around Ellen's shoulders. "We all feel like it's our fault, El. If I didn't let Beth take the kids . . . "

Let, Beth thought — *let*? You *made* me take the kids.

"I'm a bad friend," said Ellen, sobbing now. "I went out with Nick when you were in Michigan the summer of junior year . . . "

"Did you sleep with him?" Beth asked.

"No." Ellen was genuinely shocked, shocked so that her tears stopped midstream.

"Well, that's okay then," Beth said. Why were they talking about this? "You could have told me that seventy-five years ago, Ellenie."

"Why would it matter if I slept with him?"

"Because I never did."

"None of it matters," Pat put in. "We could trace this all the way back to the Korean War." He turned to Beth. "We have to go, honey. Vincent's with the Shores. We have to go by and get him . . . "

161

Both of the women turned to Pat, and, as if drilled by their combined glance, he quietly folded himself back into the car.

Ellen asked, "Where does he get off?"

"He's worn out, too, Ellenie. He just wants to get home."

"Do you?"

"Sure," she said.

Pat talked about as far as Rockford, mostly the fact that two of the new waitresses seemed to consider the cash register at Cappadora's their personal savings account. After a while, he stopped talking and sang with the radio. The baby fell asleep. Beth fell asleep, only to waken, sweating, at some minuscule shift in pressure, as if the landing gear had slid out of the bowels of the plane.

They were turning the corner onto their street. They were pulling into the driveway. The garage.

Beth had no idea how long she sat in the cave of the garage, alone.

What roused her again was her surprise at the cold, the snaky lick of cold under the summer canopy. Get up, thought Beth, and then, No, sit here a bit more. Postpone the beginning of the post-Ben period just a little more. She heard a rustle in the dark from the corner of the garage, where the snowblower was stored, and her heart did thump then. A rat. A fat, bold raccoon, waiting to bite. She threw open the car door and nearly knocked Vincent over.

"Baby!" Beth cried. "I didn't see you! Did Dad call you to come home?"

Vincent buried his face against her belly, nearly knocking Beth back into the seat. And suddenly, easily, she was holding him, too, pulling him up onto her lap.

"Mama," said Vincent, wriggling in sensuous joy. Beth froze.

She held Vincent back from her and looked at him. She had not seen him since the Fourth of July, more than a month ago, and if she were honest, not really seen him all summer. He was a leggity thing now, his last summer's shorts crowding his crotch like a bad bikini. "Mom?" Vincent asked her, wonderingly, switching back to his own word. She kissed him on both cheeks, asked him how T-ball was going, did he hit a home run? And then she set him down and picked up her purse and went into the house, Vincent skipping around and around her like a puppy.

She started to think about Bob Unger, a reporter she knew years ago at *The Capital Times*. She'd gone to Three Mile Island with him, during the meltdown crisis at the nuclear power plant. At night, after everyone filed, it was party city, war stories and card games on top of fourteen-hour work days. One night, Beth and Bob started necking in his car. She had been a tiny bit pregnant with Vincent. No one knew; they wouldn't have sent her to a place where even smart people thought it was possible to end up glowing in the dark for life. But because she was pregnant, her hormones had started to race, arousal catching her unawares. She and Pat had been having sex twice a day;

and at that moment, with hunky, prematurely gray science-guy Bob, she wanted to get down to it right there on the seat. But then Unger had slipped his hand under her sweater, and Beth suddenly sat up, smiled, punched him on the shoulder, and said, "I think we're both worn out, buddy."

She'd all but run for her room, a tumult of physical pulses at war with the big feeling — relief. Adrenaline prickles ran down both arms.

She felt that way now. Why? What had she avoided?

Vincent jumped into the house ahead of her, and Beth stopped on the threshold, steeling herself. Laurie had been here, boxing up the most obvious toys, storing some of Ben's clothes. And yet, Beth knew the house would try to take her under to the deep cold places. She would have to kick aside the bathroom stool he still used to pee. A sock would turn up, or his cowboy hat — there, right there, right now, she saw his duck umbrella against the magazine rack in the living room. Had no one else seen it? Moved it? All summer? Vincent stood in the hall, looking back at her, his thick brows drawn down, and she almost grabbed for him again, actually began to extend her arms, and he began to come forward.

But then she folded her arms back against her own body. She forced herself to smile.

What? What was it? Why couldn't she reach for her wild child and pour into him all the baby-clear affection she had felt for Ben? It wasn't Vincent's fault that Ben had never gotten old enough to sully the purity of that baby love. It would be easy, one of the right motions.

But if she did that, what would Ben have been? A sort of delayed miscarriage? No, thought Beth. No. There was no one to punish, no possibility of atonement. Only survival, through a silent celibacy of the heart. Any solace at all would be a signal to the universe that a mother could get along with one child more or less.

Oh, Ben, thought Beth, letting the door of her own house close behind her with a thud. I almost cheated on you.

9

"EIGHTY percent of us divorce," said Penny, shifting her considerable bulk to perch more comfortably on the edge of the folding chair. To be fair about it, it was a sort of pygmy chair: Beth noticed that even slight Laurie filled her seat to capacity. And Pat looked like a giant slouched on his.

Fingering the laminated button she wore that pictured her murdered four-year-old, Casey, Penny went on, "That's thirty percent more than the general population. If half of American couples divorce over the ordinary stresses of life, people who lose children the way we have lost children endure just that much more stress. And it gets you down below the surface of the water in the marriage, where the undertow is."

That's why this meeting of Compassionate Circle, Penny re-emphasized ("for the benefit of those of you joining us for the first time"), would focus on the effects of the loss on family relationships. The meeting last year on this subject, she added, flashing an astounding from-nowhere chorus girl's smile — as if the leaden door of a safe had opened in her sad, fat face — had been among the best the group had ever held.

In her own chair, the seat of honor to Penny's right, inhaling Penny's hypnotic almondy scent, Beth fantasized, and not for the first time, about the possibilities of insanity. Were she crazy, truly crazy, Penny's earnest voice would be no more than background buzz. Laurie would not have been able to drag her and Pat here. The genuinely crazy had a certain aloofness, a dignity, a madnesse-oblige. People left them alone. Did catatonics in hospitals, she wondered, really see the people they pretended to ignore, or notice the drool soaking their clothes? And did they simply refuse, from perversity, to indulge in a sentient reaction? Was true madness simply a will so ultra-strong it overcame ordinary human response? Or were such people really wandering so deep inside, on a broken landscape, so intent on minding their own footing, that the world outside receded?

That's what I want, Beth thought. To be really checked out. Few ants short of a picnic. Few bricks shy of a load. Few pickles short of a jar. One oar out of the water.

But even as she longed for it, she knew she couldn't manage it. Insanity simply managed to elude her. In a short half-hour at Compassionate Circle, two of the thirteen participants had already used the word 'breakdown' to describe their immediate circumstances following the loss of their child.

Beth didn't doubt them; she simply wanted to know, How did you do it? The best she could summon was a sort of perpetual sluggishness, in which she noticed almost everything she didn't do but almost nothing she actually did.

At first, it was just bed. Beth behaved as if she had one of the long, sheet-sweating diseases of childhood. She had her huge, delightfully full bottle of little blue footballs left over from the doctor in Chicago, and two of them sent her into a dreamless torpor for six hours at a time. When Pat came home from the restaurant before the night rush, she made sure to get up and hold the baby on her lap and look at Vincent. Then she handed the baby back to Jill and went back to bed. The children had seen her. They knew she was alive.

Soon she began to notice that she smelled. Her underwear was crusty; her oily head felt as though it were crawling with lice. So she showered, put on clean underwear and a T-shirt, and got back into bed, virtuous. If she went on like this indefinitely, would the children be able to say they had never had a mother? Of course not. They would be able to say they had a mother and she was home all the time. A stay-at-home mom, which Beth had never been. Surely Pat would never expect her to work again.

Still, she was only thirty-three. She didn't drink very often. She didn't smoke anymore, or hardly ever. Her blood pressure hovered at about a hundred and ten over seventy. Her weight was within ordinary limits. She wouldn't be running or taking aerobics classes anymore; but she had done those things for years, and thus was in relatively toned-up shape except through the hips. Her mother had died young, but that was more in the nature of an accident than the outcome of hereditary prophecy. Her grandparents had lived to great ages.

All that Kerry longevity meant that — barring unforeseen event or medical calamity, or suicide, and Beth knew she could never do it, even 'accidentally' with the blue pills — she would live her threescore and ten. She was damned if she could see what she would do with it. People would reasonably expect her to get out of bed. The thought of getting up and playing with Vincent and Kerry, or going to a supermarket or planting a bulb or frying an egg — these were outside the realm of the performable. In Chicago, she had done human things — she had driven, she had spoken — so as not to let down Candy, Ellen, Barbara Kelliher, and the band of volunteers. She could go back — consult private detectives, work harder on the solution. But she could not imagine seeing those west-side streets, ever again. Just picturing the tulip-covered yellow 'I' at the corner of the high-school driveway made her reach for her pillow and bury her head.

But a few weeks after she'd come home, Laurie brought dinner and several boxes of Ben's Missing poster to Beth's house. Beth could hear Laurie calling in the downstairs hall. She squeezed her eyes shut tight.

"I know you're awake, Beth," Laurie said, upstairs now. "I can see your eyeballs moving." Laurie sat down on the bed. "Why aren't you up?"

"I was up," Beth answered. "I just had to lie down for a minute."

"Jill says you haven't gotten out of bed in a week," Laurie replied. To this, Beth said nothing. "I know you don't feel like getting up, but you have to. Your muscles will atrophy. You'll get sores."

Beth said, "I don't care. I want my muscles to atrophy."

Laurie ran four miles four times a week, even in snow. Once, she had fallen on wet ice in front of a neighbor's house and walked up onto the woman's porch, holding the skin of her elbow together over shards of exposed bone. She'd told the woman to call 911 and sat down on the porch to wait for the ambulance. "Beth, it isn't just the inactivity. It's foolish. You don't even know what happened to him yet. If you won't talk to the TV people and you won't make phone calls, at least you can mail off some of these things to people who have called from all over the country offering to post them. It's the least you can do for Ben. I'm sorry, honey, but you're just about worthless the way you are right now."

"I don't care."

Laurie clicked her tongue once. "Beth," she said. "I've never said anything like this to you. But get the hell up, now, or I'm going to stop being your friend and then you'll be in far worse shape than you already are."

Beth swung her feet over the edge of the bed and put them on the floor.

And then, Beth did get up most mornings. The signal often was a phone call, from Candy or Laurie or Rosie. There was another body to identify; Bick had done the duty. The boy, in Gary, Indiana, was at least seven. Another call:

Did she know that there was now a billboard of Ben's face on I-90, right near the huge shopping center? Yes, Beth would reply, yes to everything, sure. And then she'd get up and brush her teeth. She might spend the whole day curled in a corner of the couch, furtively watching the street, but she did get up. Twice she went out to get the mail. The only truly ferocious moment was the early Sunday when she got up in the murky dawn light, peeked into the boys' room, and saw Ben curled up in his bed.

Pat came running when she screamed; Beth had peed her own legs.

"It's Vincent," he had explained, holding her up as she trembled. "It's just Vincent. He sleeps in Ben's bed now. He has since the night I brought him home. At first, I used to move him, but now I don't. I think . . . I think it makes him feel better, Beth. He sleeps with Ben's . . . with Ben's rabbit, Igor, too." Pat had carried her back to the bed, brought a warm wet towel and washed her, and then, somehow stimulated by the sight of her uncovered legs and hips, made love to her. Beth thought, as he gravely strained and plunged, he would get more response from screwing a basket of laundry. The children slept on. Pat's breathing was the only sound in the continuous universe.

In the middle of September, Laurie brought them to Compassionate Circle, a group she'd discovered in her PR-chick days, when Laurie had done trifolds and newsletters for almost every socially worthy organization in Madison, which was a hotbed of support programs. But the lost children of Compassionate Circle parents hadn't died of cystic fibrosis. Some of them weren't dead at all. Laurie said the catalogue of bizarre stories was truly stunning. Of them all, the group's president, Penny Odin, had the most macabre story. Her ex had picked their four-year-old son up on his birthday, phoned her an hour later, put the child on the phone, and, as he talked to his mother, shot him in the back of the head.

"Why would anybody with that kind of pain want to hear about me?" asked Beth.

"I thought maybe you might want to hear about them," Laurie suggested softly. "They say it helps to know you aren't the only one."

But, Beth thought, I am. A line from a poem snaked back to her: 'there was no other.' Mine was the only one. What did the myths and miseries and coping strategies of other busted sufferers have to do with her? She agreed to go to one meeting, only if Pat would come, too. Compassionate Circle met, as everything seemed to, in a church basement. Beth had come to think of church basements as a kind of underground railway to emotional succor — trailing all over America, where people in transformation, grieving, marrying, giving birth and dying, were gathering around scarred tables in rooms with walls covered by children's crayoned pictures of the Annunciation.

"The part of the name of our organization, Compassionate Circle, that has always meant the most to me is the word 'compass'," Penny

172

was saying now. "A compass is a circle, and it contains the four directions, north, south, east, and west, all in one circle. For many of us, there are also four emotions — joy and sorrow, knowing and mystery. For some of us, that mystery is literal. We don't know where our children are, living or dead. Even for those of us, like me, who know what happened to the child we lost, there is mystery. I believe Casey is one of the brightest singers in God's choir. But I don't know it for sure, because I haven't passed over to that plane yet. Still, every gray hair I get is a joy to me; it brings me closer to my little boy, and to our reunion." She smiled that saucy smile again — a hundred pounds ago, Beth thought, Penny must have been a looker. "Join hands now," Penny urged.

Beth wouldn't, until Laurie jerked her closed fist up from her lap.

"We meet in a circle, in the hope that healing goes around and around, as we used to sing in church when we were children," said Penny. "That's what we're here to find out, if we can have wholeness in our lives, in spite of our wounds. I think we can." She picked up a stack of pamphlets and began passing them out. "These are some of the most common problems that occur in families that lose a child. Sexual dysfunction. Acting out on the part of siblings who feel ignored or betrayed or scared. Different goals — one parent who wants to get back to business as usual and one who gets stuck . . . We've all told each other our names and the reasons we're here. Now, who

173

would like to talk about some of the matters this pamphlet suggests?"

Jean was the mother of a pregnant teenager pushed off a cliff by her older married lover. Jean almost levitated from her seat with eagerness. "When Sherry died, the turning point for me was her funeral. I went and looked at Sherry in her open coffin, and though the undertaker had done his very best, you could see from the way her muscles were all tensed up in her neck that she had been in unbelievable pain when she passed . . . "

Beth looked spears at Laurie. Was she supposed to sit here and listen to this? Laurie replied with her own shushing look, and Beth slumped in her chair, trying to lose herself in the whorls of the pattern on the pamphlet cover, a compass surrounded with rays, like the sun. "And my husband's whole goal in life," Jean went on, "was to get the man who killed her convicted. He was furious that there was no death penalty in Wisconsin, because, actually, this man killed two people, my baby and her baby. He was on the phone with the police and the lawyers all day, and I just didn't want any part of it. I mean, it wasn't going to bring Sherry back, was it? He wanted to file for compensation for us — money we would have gotten if Sherry had grown up, money for our suffering. The guy who killed her had a lot of money; he had a really good job on the line at the auto plant. I didn't even care that much about that. So, I would try to go along with him, but he could tell I wasn't really interested in it, and he started saying it

174

was because I never cared about Sherry as much as he did."

Jean and her husband were separated now, two years after her daughter's death. Jean was learning to line-dance and, for the first time in her life, was going to college, studying to be a nurse. Her husband lived in a small apartment by the lake, his only furniture a foldout bed and filing cabinets crammed with all the documents and newspaper reports on Sherry's death. It was, said Jean, a virtual shrine to Sherry — with candles that burned night and day under pictures of her all over the house. "He's going to burn himself up one day."

"Maybe he knows that," another man, Henry, put in. "I was pretty self-destructive after my wife snatched my son. In bars all the time. Picking up one woman after another. Just trying to find some softness or love. Waking up in the morning with a head the size of New Jersey . . . " Appreciative laughter rippled around the table.

A very young woman, who had not let go of her husband's hand for the entire duration of the meeting — which Beth noticed, with dismay, was now almost ninety minutes — spoke up then. "You know," she said, "I'm wondering if there's something wrong with us, because we really haven't experienced any of those problems. Jenny's death just brought us closer, closer to each other and closer to God." Jenny, the couple's two-year-old, had been crushed under the wheels of her caregiver's car as the woman (who was, unbeknownst to her employers, drunk) backed out of the driveway one night after work. "We've found that whenever one of us needs a shoulder to cry on, the other one is always there. We look at Jenny's pictures, and though of course we're sad, and we'll always be sad, we try to remember the joy she brought us, and we find that very healing. We were lucky to have had her."

Laurie wrote on the corner of her pamphlet, shoving it noiselessly across to Beth: 'They probably didn't want kids to begin with.' Beth covered her face with one hand.

"So, we're finding that this experience," the young mother went on, "difficult as it is, has actually been a time of growing . . . so that when we have another child, and we're sure we will — "

"Why are you here, then?" Henry asked bitterly. "If you're doing so great, how come you want to come and be with people who aren't doing so great?"

"Henry," Penny reminded him gently. "You know the covenants of the Circle. We don't begrudge and we don't grudge. Everyone has a right to work through a loss in their own way . . . "

"But they don't seem like they need any help," Henry said.

"But we do," said the woman. "We need to know that we're not alone."

"Of course you do," said Penny, turning suddenly to Beth. "Now, our newest guests, Pat and Beth, are just starting along the road some of us have been on for a long time. All of you have read about Ben Cappadora, Beth's

176

little boy. We have every reason to believe that your son will be found, Beth, but your family must be experiencing some of these reactions of mourning. Do you feel like talking about it?"

"No," said Beth, and then, surprising herself, she asked, "How did you get how you are?"

Penny looked puzzled. "How did I . . . ?"

"How you are. So accepting. So kind. Were you always like that? I mean, before?"

Penny nearly laughed. "I sure wasn't. The first few months after Casey was shot by my ex-husband, the only thing I allowed myself to feel was rage. Rage at my own stupidity for trusting my ex-husband with my son, because I knew he was strung out about half the time. Rage at the man himself, for doing what he did. I quit going to church, and I devoted myself to eating everything in the house that wasn't nailed down . . . " She gestured to her bright red tunic. "You can see the results of that. If you would have told me that I'd ever feel any different, I'd have said you were a fool, you just never understood what I'd been through . . . "

"So how?" Beth asked again, feeling a rush of admiration, a wish to graft some piece of Penny's peace under the skin of her own heart.

"Well, what I did, Beth, was . . . I finally forced myself to . . . do things like look at the pictures of Casey after he died," Penny said, with the first trace of hesitancy Beth had heard in her voice all night, "Casey was shot at pointblank range in the back of the head. And I forced myself to think, What did he feel? What did he know? And the answer was, he knew nothing. He was talking to me, and then he was gone, just gone. When I looked at it from Casey's point of view, I had to think that he died, but he died happy and painlessly and quickly, and that the person it hurt most wasn't him. It was me. And my . . . and my ex-husband. Because Wisconsin isn't a death-penalty state, he has to live with this forever, even now that he's sober."

"And you feel sorry for him? Does he get some kind of pass because he's crazy?" Beth asked.

"I guess, no, I don't feel sorry for him," Penny said. "I do feel, though, that his regret and grief are a kind of justice."

Beth looked up. Pat was on his feet. He hadn't said a word beyond his name all night, but he now said, "I'm so sorry. I can't stand anymore."

"I understand. Do come back," said Penny. "Anytime. Any time you want. Or call me."

"I will," Beth said.

Outside, the last of the light was draining from a perfectly transparent fall sky. Beth breathed in, heavily, the smells of the church's patch of wild roses, the bus exhaust from the metro on its way up Park Street.

Laurie asked Pat, "Are you okay?"

He said, "I just felt as though I couldn't . . . I never imagined there was so much suffering in the world."

Oh, Pat, Beth thought, there just never was in yours.

But that night, she couldn't forget Penny Odin's foolish, saintly face. Did Penny sleep?

Beth got up and walked into the boys' room and stood over Vincent as he lay curled on Ben's bed. Each of the boys had a shelf over the head of his bed for books and toys; each one had a designated side to the closet, neatly labeled with stick-up letters spelling out their names.

Laurie had done her work sensitively and well. Only a few discreet things hung well back in Ben's side of the closet. His toys were mostly gone (also boxed and stored in the crawl space, Beth knew, out of sight but not forgotten). There had been an easing of Ben's imprint, a consolidation, but not a clean sweep. Thank you, my dear Laurie, Beth thought, kneeling down at Vincent's side. Thank you for letting me be able to come in here.

Vincent had always slept hard. She had never seen him wake easily; he was like a cold-cocked prizefighter — he woke disoriented, bleary, looking plucked as a newly hatched chick. But now he rolled in his sleep, twitching, sweating like a racer. Maybe he's sick, she thought. He'd asked her a lot of odd questions since she came home.

"How many bad guys are there in Madison?" he had asked. Vincent wasn't the kind of child to be fobbed off with something easy.

She'd said, to get it over with, "There are thirty."

"Are you sure?"

"Yes."

"Who said?"

"Detective Bliss. She counted."

179

"How many are there in Los Angeles?" he'd asked then.

Beth had sighed. "There are two hundred," she'd told him.

What he was really asking was, Am I next? Beth knew that. What could she tell him? What could she feel, in front of his asking eyes, except accused and resentful? Hadn't she let the bough break?

A memory, a safe one, flitted past her face like moth wings. Just before Ben was born, Vincent had stared at her belly and said, "You'll like the baby. But it won't be the same. You won't like the baby as much as you like me." And Beth had feared the same thing.

Indeed, Ben had managed to perfect for himself the role of second child, undemanding and delighted, the one she knew she would never need to worry about, never need to worry about . . . and she hadn't.

She hadn't worried at all.

Now she should be worrying. About Vincent. But it was all gone, that mother radar, along with her belief in it. She could do nothing for Vincent. Leaning low, she whispered, "I love you." Studies had shown that even in deep sleep, people could hear, could even learn languages that came to them on paths of the subconscious. Perhaps it would work, and he would wake up feeling loved, even if he wasn't sure who loved him. Or whether she was still around.

10

Vincent

December 1985

VINCENT had thought it over and he decided he would ask Santa for Ben. What he really wanted was a Lionel train or a radio-controlled boat, but the way he figured it was, if he asked Santa for Ben, he might get the boat and the train, too, because asking for Ben was an unselfish wish. Santa would be impressed, and everyone would be happy. His mother. Grandpa Angelo. Everybody.

Vincent would probably be happy, too, because, to tell the truth, after six months, he was getting sick of not having Ben around. Kerry was cute, but you couldn't really play with her yet. Plus she was a little smelly and boring. And his mother was still acting like she was sick, sitting around all the time, except once in a while yelling at him if he got too loud. It wasn't like she never yelled at him before Ben got lost; but in between yelling, she used to do stuff with him and be funny. Now when he tried to make her laugh by singing Elvis or something, she didn't even notice. He had the feeling that getting Ben back for Christmas would be about the only thing that would make her goof around. The way things were now was annoying.

Back in Chicago, he hadn't minded because he could do anything he wanted. He never had to go back to school for the last week before summer break, and he still got passed into second, and got almost all Es, even though he was pretty sure he was only going to get an S in math because he goofed with Andrew P. the whole time. His teacher even wrote him a note and sent him some Geoffrey dollars. There was a lot more hugging and petting him than Vincent strictly liked, some of it from old people whose breath smelled like the wooden sticks the doctor used to hold your tongue down. But the police gave him all kinds of stuff — baseball cards, a play badge that was real metal and wouldn't break if you left it on your shirt when it went into the washing machine, and so much gum he had to make a special place in a drawer to store it all. The lady with the blond hair who was a police officer even though she was really pretty gave him a piece of the stuff bulletproof vests were made out of. Grandma Rosie sewed it inside his Batman shirt for him. (He later put on that shirt and his dad's fishing hat for Halloween, until Alex's mother picked him up to go trick-or-treating. She took him back to her house to put some face paint on him, all the while saying to Alex's dad, "Enough's enough — really, enough's enough" — like face paint was that expensive.)

But at first, he liked that everybody who came over gave him something. Grandpa Bill's friends gave him dollars, paper and silver ones. He saved up eleven dollars the first week. And when he whined and wouldn't eat, they just took the plate away and gave him anything — cookies, or even the kind of cereal his mother wouldn't let him have, the kind with little marshmallow people in it. Uncle Bick even went out at night to get it at the store, just because Vincent wanted it . . . which actually almost gave Vincent the creeps.

It made him wonder if they were all telling him the truth, and whether Ben was really killed instead of alive but not here. And letting him have anything he wanted actually made him miss his mom even more, and he already missed his mom a lot. She was never around when they were in Chicago. Sometimes she called up and said, "Hi, Vincent." His dad was around more often, but had this new, really hard way of hugging him that was also creepy.

All in all, though, Chicago was better. Grandpa Angelo used to put him in their big cannonball bed at night to sleep — not just the first night, *every* night. And even when he couldn't sleep, people were talking out in the living room. Police and grownups.

Now, at home, when he couldn't sleep, he just sort of sat there. His mother never made any noise at night. Kerry never made any noise. Unless it was Monday, his dad was always gone at the restaurant at bedtime. Vincent hated just sitting. He understood now why adults knew how to read fast. A long time ago, he and Ben used to figure out quiet ways of getting out of bed and playing with their cars until they started hitting and laughing and somebody caught them.

But Vincent was afraid to do it on his own. It just seemed really dangerous to disobey, even though he was pretty sure his mom wouldn't even notice.

Getting to sleep had always been Vincent's best thing. His mother used to say, "You're the best sleeper of all." All you did was shut your eyes and float, like you were in a big, warm tub. But since the thing happened in the lobby, Vincent couldn't just fall asleep anymore. For one thing, he had the room to himself now; and though he liked being able to spread his stuff out on both beds, it felt weird having nobody to talk to at night. For another thing, he was all of a sudden almost afraid of the dark. It wasn't just one of those things kids feel. He had a good reason to be scared. After all, the kidnapper would probably come and get him, too. It made sense. That kind of bad guy, the kind they told you about at school, who would come up and ask you for directions and grab your arm right in front of your own house, and give you drugs and touch you inappropriately, would definitely want the other brother, too. And if the bad guy asked, Ben would say where Vincent was. Ben knew the number of their house.

Vincent got so nervous, he told Uncle Joey about it, and Uncle Joey said no bad guys better dare ever come near Grandpa's house or he would take them out.

"Do you know what that means, buddy, 'take them out'?" Uncle Joey said in a rough voice. And Vincent had nodded his head, though he didn't; but Uncle Joey was a bodybuilder, so he figured it meant he would punch the bad guys.

But people always said stuff like that to kids, didn't they?

They said you would always be safe, and they would keep you safe, but then you could fall on the playground toys and break your collarbone with them standing right there. You could get kidnapped in front of a million people. And the bad guy probably didn't even need to give Ben drugs or candy. He probably just told him what to do, because kids like Ben did what grownups told them. Even Vincent, who usually didn't, even he sometimes did what certain adults told him to, like when his mom told him to eat eggs, even though eggs made him want to barf.

Once, before they came home, he dreamed that who took Ben was a witch, like in 'Hansel and Gretel'. Grandma Rosie said there were no such things as witches. Vincent didn't really believe her. It was just another sort of lie adults told kids to make them not be scared. If there were no witches, how come there used to be in the olden times? When all those stories were written? Where did they all go to? Didn't they have babies who grew up to be witches?

There was also the third thing. The smell thing.

It was the only thing he really remembered about the day Ben got lost, that smell. And he couldn't really smell it; he could just remember it. Like all the different powders and perfumes in Mom's makeup bag, all mixed, and then this stinky cooking smell. Uncle Augie would say in a restaurant that wasn't owned by somebody they knew, "Bottle gravy." Like at Thanksgiving, when his mother had opened up a jar of turkey gravy because they forgot to bring gravy from the restaurant — it was just like that smell. It made Vincent so sick he couldn't eat anything, and his dad said quit trying to always be the center of attention, and his mom said shut up about it, and she didn't eat either. She took him upstairs and lay down on the bed with him, which was actually pretty nice. He had no trouble going to sleep that time, and they slept all day.

Most of the time, though, his mother didn't put him to bed or wake him up. She put the baby in bed and said, "Night-night, Kerry," and then she would just stand there in the hall, for so long, with her hand on the knob of baby Kerry's door.

Vincent would get his pajamas on and come back out there. Then he would brush his teeth and come back out there. After a while, he would go and get in bed. He didn't know if it was his bedtime, because he couldn't tell time on the upstairs clocks, only the one on the VCR that had actual numbers. A few times, he didn't get up in time for school, either, but when he told his teacher that his mother forgot to wake him up, they said it was okay, they wouldn't mark him tardy. After a while, a couple of times, he didn't go even when he knew it was time, when he could see other kids going to school on the street. He just watched TV until his mother came down with the baby.

She just said, "Did you eat?" She didn't ask

him, 'Aren't you supposed to be in school?' Once she asked, "Is it Sunday?" That time, he got up and left. They were halfway through journals when he got there, but his teacher didn't say anything except ask him if he had any breakfast. Vincent said no, and the teacher's face got all hard, like she was going to cry. She gave him part of a doughnut. After that, he just said he ate.

After school, he mostly went to Alex's. He had heard Alex's mother say, on the phone, "Yes, of course, Vincent's here, too. I'm filing the adoption papers next week." And he had to ask his dad if Alex's parents were really going to adopt him. His dad told him, "Of course not," and said, "Maybe you should come home some days after school."

But Vincent didn't like to get home too early. Not until Jill got done with classes. The baby would be asleep. And his mom would be sitting in funny places. Once down in the basement in her darkroom, on the floor in the dark, but not doing anything. Once in his bedroom, next to the bed that used to be Ben's but was now his. Once right in the kitchen, on the floor. That was the scariest time. She had a cup of coffee next to her that had scummy stuff on top and a bug stuck in the scummy stuff, and he'd had to yell, "Mom, ick! Don't drink that!" because when she saw him, she picked it up and started to drink it. And she'd tried to laugh then, a sort of scary heh-heh laugh. And she just put the cup back down on the floor and sat there.

But even if he went to Alex's right after

school, he couldn't eat over every night. He had to come home when Alex's dad got back from work, which was about five o'clock. There were times, of course, when he didn't go to Alex's at all.

To get to Alex's house, he had to pass his own house on the other side of the street. And there were some afternoons that he could see that somebody's car was in the driveway, like Laurie, who would probably have one of her kids with her, and the kid and Vincent would go play in the treehouse or have jumping contests off the swings.

And even if one of the kids wasn't with her, when Laurie was there it was like his mom woke up. It was like they turned on her remote control or something. She answered things when they said them, and if they had to sit around and mail and stamp packages of Ben's Wanted poster, Mom would do that right along with Laurie. If Laurie brought a salad for her, his mom would eat it. She would make coffee. She would seem to see Vincent, too, when Laurie or a neighbor was there. She would say, "Would you get me the stapler, big buddy?" in a voice that sounded almost like her old voice, except if you had actually heard her old voice you knew that this one was a toy version, a lot faster and smaller.

Those nights, things would be really great, because by the time Laurie left, Jill would be there, and she would warm up whatever Laurie brought for dinner — not that he didn't love the food from Cappadora's, but you liked to have

American food once in a while, too, like fried chicken. That would be a whole day, from the end of school until bed, when he didn't have to be alone with his mom, if it was one of the nights when Jill didn't have a night class, which she did three times a week. But if she didn't, she would read to him and run a bath for him and even stay in his room until he fell asleep.

Once, he woke up in the middle of the night and Jill was still right there, sleeping on the bed that used to be his with her clothes still on and no covers. Vincent got up and put the comforter over her, trying to fit it up around her shoulders without waking her up. But she woke up anyway, and hugged him. He felt awful then; he was afraid she'd leave. But she just turned over and went back to sleep. Vincent liked that so much he told Jill she could sleep there any time she wanted, instead of the guest room she lived in. But when he said that, Jill started to cry, so he didn't tell her it again. His bed was not as comfortable as Ben's, it was true. His mattress was older, because Ben had peed his to death and he got a new one, and Vincent's had a major saggy place in the middle. He didn't really blame Jill.

Vincent knew Jill was going to go home to her real home, with her mother, his auntie Rachelle, for Christmas anyhow. She'd be gone a whole month. Dad said Stacey, the cashier from Cappadora's, was going to baby-sit him and Kerry some nights "until Mom feels better." Stacey wasn't really mean or anything, but all she ever did was watch TV. And she wasn't going to come every night. Even when she did come, she wasn't going to be there at ten o'clock at night, after his mom and the baby were asleep and his dad wasn't home yet.

That was the part Vincent dreaded, being up when his mom was asleep.

By the time vacation started, a week before Christmas, Vincent had his routine pretty well figured out. He could look forward to Monday nights being pretty good, because Dad was home; Tuesday and Wednesday nights would be pretty bad; Thursdays okay because by that time of the week, one of Mom's friends usually was starting to call to see if she was okay; Friday would be okay. Saturday okay about half the time because he could usually talk his dad into taking him to the restaurant and letting him fall asleep on the couch in Uncle Augie's office.

Sundays were the worst. Dad had to open, and so he left right after lunch. He always looked really upset when he left. He kept saying, "Beth? You're all right now, aren't you?"

And his mother would say, "Sure. I'm fine." Then she would watch out the window when his dad left, like she could still see his car pulling down the driveway backwards an hour after he left. A few times, Vincent asked her if he could go out to play. She said, "Okay." But Vincent didn't; he didn't feel too good about going out to play, even if there was new snow, until Kerry was down for her nap. If she threw all her toys out of the playpen, his mom wouldn't put them back. Vincent did, even though it drove him nuts that Kerry would just throw them out again.

190

On Sundays, the phone would ring all day. Sometimes, his mom would pick it up. Sometimes, she wouldn't. A couple of times, after she picked it up, he heard her yelling swear words — like "You sick buster!" — and then she called his dad and he had to come home from the restaurant so his mom could go to bed. His dad was pretty upset when that happened, and once he even called the police in Madison.

So Vincent answered the phone most of the time now.

Often the person who called would be Detective Bliss, who said to call her 'Candy'. Or the lady from Compassionate Circle. Or Uncle Bick. Uncle Bick always made him actually get his mother, even if Vincent said she was asleep, and he could also make her talk, even if in just one words.

Two times, though, it was a man Vincent didn't know. Except he knew it was the same man. He sounded like he was calling from a room with all the sounds sealed out of it, a room that didn't even have normal noises in the back, like TV or cars going by. He asked, "Are you the brother of the little boy?"

Vincent told him, "Yes."

And the man asked, "Do you know why he was stolen?"

Vincent said, "No."

The man said then, real whispery, "Do you know how our Lord Jesus Christ punishes sinners? That he who disturbeth his own house shall reap the whirlwind?"

It wasn't what he said that scared Vincent, but

how angry he sounded. Mad at Vincent. Like Vincent was the one who stole Ben. Vincent tried to tell him, "My mommy's asleep," even though that embarrassed him a little, because he usually didn't say 'mommy' anymore; but the guy just kept right on, hissing, "Do you know about Benjamin in the Bible, son? Vanished into slavery in Egypt? Do you know what sick people do to little boys like your brother?"

The one time, Vincent called his mother, and something in his voice made her shake her head and sit up — she had been watching a bass-fishing show that he was pretty sure she wasn't really interested in. "What?" she said. "What?" He just held the phone out and shook it. And his mother took it and when she heard the man, she really yelled, "Don't you ever call my house again, you — " *f* word, *a* word, *p* word.

The next time the man called, Vincent just said, "I believe in God," and hung up. The man called back and left sixteen messages. "Pick up the phone, if you want to know what really happened to Benjamin," he kept saying. Sixteen times. Vincent counted. Then he never called back again. Vincent figured it was the kidnapper. But when his dad heard the tape he said it wasn't; it was just a sick buster who had nothing better to do with his sick life than scare women and children. He gave the tape to the police in Madison. They came over to the house in a squad car to get it.

Vincent started to think he could tell whether it was a good call or a bad call by the ring. If it was Aunt Tree or somebody, Vincent thought he could hear a kind of friendly bounce in the ring. If it was police or strangers or guys wanting to sell his parents some graves or houses or something, it would have sort of a distant sound, as if it didn't really know where it was ringing. So he tried to only pick up when he heard the bounce, and by Christmas vacation he had determined that he was right about twenty times out of twenty-five; he kept count by making a little tiny ink mark on the bottom of the kitchen table where they put the raw, crummy wood that didn't have the gray covering on top. It was entirely possible that he had ESP.

Usually it was Grandma Rosie who called.

Grandma would say, "Is your mama there, Vincenzo?"

And Vincent would say, "Yes. She's sleeping." Even if she wasn't. Because if he gave his mom the phone, she would just hold it and listen to Grandma Rosie, hardly saying anything, and he would hear Grandma Rosie's little phone voice getting louder and louder on the other end. Which made him want to jump out of his skin, because he couldn't really tell his mom to say something.

When Vincent told Grandma that his mom was sleeping, though, that was another problem. She would say, "Hmmmmmm." He could hear her tapping on the table with her little silver pen, the one she used to write orders at the Golden Hat. Then she would say, "Where is the baby?"

And he would say, "Sleeping, too." Even if *she* wasn't. He could tell that was what

Grandma Rosie wanted Kerry to be doing, because people always thought babies were better off sleeping. Then Grandma Rosie would ask if he was watching television. She would ask him to spell a couple of words — usually, two easy, like 'ran' or 'fat', and one hard, like 'nose' or 'high', which could fool you. She would say, "I was thinking my car might come up to Madison this weekend. But Grandpa said no, too many people getting married this weekend. Everybody's getting married on the west side, 'Cenzo." She said that almost every time. Except just the past week, she was saying, "Soon we will be there for Christmas," and asking if Vincent had been a good boy, and what Saint Nicholas would bring for him.

That was when he told her he was asking for Ben.

He could tell right away Grandma Rosie didn't like the idea. She said, "Oh, Vincenzo. *Carissimo*." Like he had said he got suspended for fighting or something. Vincent had actually expected her to be proud of him, and have her voice get all purry, the way it did when he sent her the recital tape the first year he took Suzuki violin. But, he figured, probably she was just tired. He asked to talk to Grandpa Angelo. Grandpa would probably like the idea better; he was really missing Ben. Grandpa said it made his heart feel like a bone in his throat or something — Vincent couldn't exactly remember the way he described it. But Grandpa hadn't been home. And Grandma Rosie got off the phone really quick.

Vincent thought he'd have to tell Dad, and see if Dad would help him with the letter to Santa. He didn't want to tell his mom.

Christmas Eve was going to be on a Monday, and on the Friday night before, Uncle Paul called to tell Vincent's mom they'd be up that night. Then, Vincent started getting really excited. Uncle Paul's twins, especially Moira, were really nuts and rough, for girls; he always had a good time with them. "Can the twins sleep in my room?" he asked Uncle Paul. "I have an extra bed now that Ben's gone."

There was a long pause, in which Vincent could hear somebody's car phone or radio click in and out on the line. "Uh, okay," said Uncle Paul. "Let me talk to your mom."

Grandpa Angelo and Grandma Rosie arrived Saturday morning. Vincent's dad had to make three trips to the car to bring in all the presents. Vincent began to read the gift tags on the packages out loud: 'To Kerry, from Santa'. 'To Beth, F.U.F.I.L.' (that sounded like a swear, but Grandpa Angelo did it all the time; it meant 'From you father-in-law', and it was funny because Grandpa had an Italian accent). Then there were a whole stack of boxes that said, 'To Ben from Grandma and Grandpa'. 'To Ben from Santa'.

Vincent followed Grandpa Angelo out into the kitchen. "Grandpa," he said. "You made a mistake. These are for Ben, and you know, Ben is kidnapped right now . . . "

Grandpa's eyes got all red in the white part. "I know, 'Cenzo," he said, squatting down,

195

"But Grandma and me, we think if we keep on believing that our Benbo will come back to us, the Lord will answer our prayers, And so we buy him gifts, so we don't forget our Ben, and so he will have them when he comes home."

"I'm going to show my mom."

"Okay," said Grandpa Angelo. "In a little while." He looked around. "Where's the Christmas tree?"

Vincent felt bad. He knew that he could have told his dad that nobody had remembered to put up a Christmas tree; but he was afraid his dad would cry if he did. So Vincent ran upstairs without answering Grandpa and got his mom. She usually didn't come down until around lunchtime, but she came right down today, and she had on normal clothes instead of her red Badger sweat pants with the holes in them, the ones she slept in and wore all day. She had on black pants and a white shirt tucked in. Vincent was proud of her. She kissed everybody.

"Mom," Vincent said, tugging on her arm, "I want to show you something special."

But he didn't get to show her Ben's presents right then, because Aunt Tree and Uncle Joey drove up. Aunt Tree told everybody she didn't know whether she should come or not, because she was starting to have breaks and hicks. Vincent assumed this had something to do with Aunt Tree's baby, still in her tummy, and he was right.

"Ahhhhh," Grandma Rosie said. "Maybe a Christmas baby!"

196

"They have hospitals right here in Madison, Tree-o," Dad said.

"Little early yet," said Grandpa Angelo.

"Just a few days," Grandma said. "Easier, anyhow, if it's a little early. Her first one." Aunt Monica wasn't coming, because she was spending Christmas with a boyfriend. Even though she had long nails and could play the piano, Aunt Monica didn't have a husband yet; she always told Vincent he was the only man she could count on.

Aunt Tree couldn't run upstairs, and she hadn't wrapped all her presents yet, so she made Vincent her 'lieutenant', telling him to get her the tape and the ribbon shredder. And then, just when he was about to show his mom the gifts for Ben, suddenly Dad's buddy Rob came with a tree — an already decorated tree!

Vincent smelled it, and it wasn't fake. Rob said Delilo's Florists had given it to Dad for free. The tree made everything look better. Everybody took a long time putting the presents under it. Vincent went to get his Playskool tape recorder, to hide under the tree behind some of the packages. He planned to turn it on right before he went to bed, in case he couldn't stay awake long enough, so that he could tape Santa. He figured that if he could be the first kid in America to actually prove there was a real Santa, he could get on TV. He'd told Jill about this idea, and she told him it was excellent. Tonight would be a test. If he could hear what the grownups said on his tape after he was in bed, at least until it clicked off, then he knew he'd catch Santa for sure.

Rob stayed for a glass of wine, and Aunt Sheilah had already taken the twins up to bed by the time Vincent finally got the chance to tell his mother about the gifts for Ben. She was sitting on the couch, holding a cup of coffee but not drinking it, and he walked up to her quietly and said, "Look, Mom. All those presents are for Ben. Grandpa and Grandma brought them. Wasn't that nice?"

Grandma Rosie was sitting across from Mom, embroidering on a picture she was making for Aunt Tree's baby, and Mom didn't even look at Vincent. She just walked over to the tree and held up one of the packages and said, real flat, "Rosie."

Even to Vincent, Grandma looked up as if she was guilty, like she'd been caught passing notes in school with the word 'piss' written on them. "Bethie?" she asked softly. "What, dear?"

"What are these?"

"Presents for Ben."

"You brought presents for Ben."

"Yes."

"Rosie, why did you bring presents for Ben?"

"Because," Grandma Rosie said, in her talking-to-a-kid voice, "I believe that Ben will be found. And I want him to know that his family didn't forget him, when he is found."

"Do you have the impression that we have forgotten Ben?"

"No, my dear."

"But we didn't get Ben any presents."

"I understand that."

"In fact," said Mom, "to tell you the truth, I didn't even want to have this whole . . . go through this whole big holiday act. I didn't want to do anything except sleep through it. And when you do this, when you act like he's just out of town on a business trip and he'll be back anytime, Rosie, do you know what that does to me?" Her voice was getting loud, and Vincent heard the chairs scrape as his dad and Rob got up in the kitchen and came out to see what was the matter.

"Beth," Grandma Rosie was saying, "no one meant to upset you."

"But you *knew* it would upset me."

"Bethie," said Vincent's dad, "please. You know what they said in the Circle. Everyone needs a ritual."

"But I don't, Pat!" Vincent's mother was crying now. "And I'm his mother! I don't want to do a bunch of stupid things to pretend that my baby is alive and on his way home, when that's the cruelest lie in the world! I don't want to rub my face in all this shit!"

"Beth honey!" Aunt Tree said then. "Take it easy. Ma didn't mean anything."

"Take it easy? Take it easy?" his mother cried. "How can I take it easy when nobody except me seems to want to accept that this is over — it's *over*? And we're just all going to go on acting the way we always have, eating and sleeping and baptizing babies . . . "

"What's my baby got to do with this?" Aunt Tree asked, grabbing her tummy; she was mad. "Listen, Beth. You've got to snap out of it at some point. No one can talk to you. I can't. Pat can't. If you don't have any hope at all that Ben will come back — "

"Come back? He's not even four yet! What's he going to do? Get an Amtrak schedule?"

"What I mean, Beth, is that if the rest of Ben's family wants to keep up hope, that's our business. It's not an insult to you. And furthermore, Beth, what do you care? How does it affect you? You're an . . . island, Beth. You don't care even care about my baby . . . "

"No. I don't."

"Well, you should. Life goes on."

"If I never hear anyone say 'Life goes on' again, it'll be too soon, Teresa." That was a first. Vincent had forgotten Aunt Tree's real name.

"And you don't care about my mother or my father, and the fact that they're as knocked out by this as you are. And that they don't know what to make of how you're behaving. Now, I have to admit, I would be curled up on the floor. I couldn't go on like you do. But you have withdrawn from the whole family. And that's okay, but if you do that, you can't control — "

"Tree," Vincent's dad warned, very tired. "Tree, wait — "

"No, Pat. You're all too scared to say this, but I'm not! We try to call, she won't talk to us. We write, she won't answer us. We can't talk about anything in our lives that doesn't have to do with Beth's grief. She's like Deirdre, Mother of Sorrows — nothing in the world can ever be

200

as bad as what she's going through, so she's just opted out of life completely."

"That's right. That's my choice."

"But it isn't *ours*, Beth. You don't own every choice about Ben. He was ours, too. And we haven't decided to give up. We still go over at night and mail bunches of leaflets to people in New York and Kansas and Oklahoma. We still talk to the police. We still want to believe that there's hope, and you can't stop us, and I don't know why you want to, because you aren't going to find him by sitting on your duff all day and — "

That was when Vincent decided he had to tell his mom that there was a very good chance things were going to be fine by Christmas morning, that Ben would be back.

"Mom," he said, "I have to tell you what I did." He wondered if, actually, this was going to be sort of a lie, because he hadn't actually written a Santa letter. He had simply tried praying to Santa, because Grandma Rosie insisted he was a saint and you could pray to saints any time you wanted; they were up there waiting for it. So he took a deep breath and said, "Wait a minute, Mom. I asked Santa to bring Ben home. I think he'll do it."

It was like freeze tag.

Nobody in the room moved. Nobody spoke.

Then his mom got up and carefully put down her cup and dug her hands up under the roots of her hair and stumbled out of the room toward the stairs. Vincent looked at his dad. Once, on Mother's Day a couple of months after Kerry

201

was born, he and his dad had brought his mother a whole basket full of wild roses, and she had put her face right down into them and cried and cried, and when Vincent asked why, his father told him, "She's happy, Vincent. I know it sounds funny, but sometimes adults get so happy that they cry."

Was that it?

Grandma Rosie was leaning her head on Aunt Tree's shoulder. Grandpa Angelo got up, jingling his car keys, and said he was going to take a ride over to the restaurant and see Augie. Vincent's dad picked him up and said, "I think it's time for bed, slugger. Just a few days until Christmas. Gotta get your rest." Vincent struggled to get down. Why was everyone mad at him? Did they think it was mean to ask Santa for your own brother? But even though for once he was glad to go to bed, he wanted to switch on his tape first. "I just want to look at that one big present, Dad," he lied.

When they were up in his room, and his father had bounced him on Ben's bed and laid him down and sung a couple of verses of 'Davy Crockett', Vincent asked, "Remember that one time when all I did was bop Ben on the head very softly and he bit me?"

"Yeah. I put Ben in our room to separate you."

"When it was actually Ben's fault."

"Well, you did bop him."

"Very softly. And he bit me very, very hard."

"He liked to bite. But he stopped that after he got bigger."

"Yeah," said Vincent. "I just wanted you to know, Dad, I forgive him for that."

"Good," said his dad. "I'm glad. Now, go to sleep. The twins are already out. They're good little girls, not sneaky little monkeys who run around all night. Don't you dare wake them up." He kissed Vincent and said, "I love you."

"Where's Mom?" Vincent asked then.

"She's in her room."

"Is she sick?"

"A little, yeah. A little bit. Even grownups have fights sometimes, Vincent. You know that. It'll all be better in the morning."

But in the morning, it only got worse, because instead of talking loud at each other, everyone was so polite. At least the tape had worked pretty well. He heard his dad say to his aunt, " . . . the amount of stress. And she doesn't answer it because she thinks half the time it's going to be the police saying they've found another kid or some nut trying to tell her we killed him."

"But even given all that, Paddy, she needs professional help. She really needs professional help."

"Maybe," said his dad. "Yeah."

Then they started to talk about Monica being stuck up and all kinds of stuff Vincent didn't even care about.

But professional help. That, thought Vincent, was a great idea. He hoped his dad really meant it. If his mom had a professional helper, someone who did helping for a job, right in the house all the time, she would have to wash and change her clothes every day, because the helper would make her. She would have to change Kerry more often, so that Kerry didn't soak through the front of her little sleepers every day before Jill got home. Vincent couldn't change diapers, because Kerry was too wiggly; he'd tried, and she just rolled over and over until she was away from him. His mom had to do it. If the helper could get his mom moving, so she did more things without taking forever, she would have more time, because as far as Vincent could tell, she wasn't doing her picture work anymore at all. They could maybe take walks. Maybe make a mobile; she used to like to make mobiles out of wire hangers and cut-out stars. He might be too big for that now, but he didn't care. He'd do it if his mom wanted to. And after a while of doing normal things again, she would start to realize that even if Ben was gone right now, she still had even more kids than she'd lost. She had double the number of kids she'd lost.

And he was pretty sure he and Kerry together made up for one Ben. Maybe even one and a half.

11

Beth

NOT long after the *People* magazine landed on the stands, seven months to the day after Ben was taken, Candy passed through Madison, unannounced, on the way to a forensics conference in Michigan. Beth later believed she had made a special detour; it was like Candy to anticipate how Beth would feel when she saw the cover, which was a full-page bleed of the second Missing poster, with no headline other than '1-800-FIND BEN' and a little kicker that said, 'Before Their Very Eyes: The Strange Disappearance of Ben Cappadora.' No teases on movie stars' pregnancies or stories about diet doctors. Just Ben.

Laurie had brought it to the house the day it came out.

Beth wouldn't talk to her, even after Pat pleaded through the locked bedroom door. Finally, Laurie told Pat to go away. "Bethie, listen," she said. "You're going to hate me for this, and I know it. But it's been a long time now, Beth. The police are getting nowhere." Beth could hear Laurie lightly rubbing the door, as if she were patting Beth on the back. Laurie went on, "You see that magazine at every doctor's office in America, Bethie. And when that reporter called me, well, I decided that I was going to talk to her even though I knew what you'd think. It was the right thing to do, Bethie. I love you. I love Ben. And I've just always thought this paranoia about the media was ... unreasonable. So, even if you never speak to me again, I'm glad I did it. And you should know, Barbara talked to them, too. And so did Wayne. And so did your sister-in-law Teresa. And if you hate them, too, I'm sorry for you. Beth, when you're ready, I'll be waiting to talk to you." Beth could hear Laurie's silent presence outside the door, like a drawn breath. "Okay, Beth. 'Bye now."

The magazine was on the floor outside Beth's bedroom door when she opened it an hour later. She sat down, right there, in the opening between the lintels, and flipped to page sixty, thinking, absurdly, They always make you wait for the cover story, no matter what it is, they make you wade through sixteen things about the ninth-grade genius who figured out how to make a computer out of a clock radio, or the model who had two babies in eighteen months and starved herself back to perfect flatitude in six weeks.

She thought she could read the first paragraph. That, she would allow herself, though she could feel the cold and crush shimmering above her even as she folded back the facing page, the one covered with photographs she barely glanced at but couldn't help recognize. She'd taken most of them herself, after all — a Christmas photo of her three kids that had been the centerpiece of a card: newborn Kerry, Vincent, and Ben in Santa hats, all of them with their tongues sticking out. A picture on Laurie's picnic table of Ben and Laurie's son in clown makeup. Laurie had that one framed in her living room.

On the first page, it was just the first Wanted poster. Beth could look at that — she'd seen it so often that it had finally become meaningless. She no longer wanted to claw her wrists when she looked at the cockeyed tilt of Ben's baseball cap, the crease in his nose when he smiled. And down below, a glamorous shot of Candy talking to reporters outside the Parkside station, looking up, clearly irritated by the photographer, but still every-hair-perfect despite the grim set of her jaw.

Okay, thought Beth. You can read one line. Two. 'When Beth Cappadora took her children to the fifteenth reunion of her high-school class in Chicago, she expected a time of togetherness with old friends, not the beginning of a nightmare that would tear apart a family, old friendships, and the very fiber of a community . . . ' Beth slapped the covers together.

She knew what the rest would entail — a couple thousand words of breezy, bathetic prose wrapped around pictures that would make even women waiting for mammograms count their blessings as they read. Enough. It was done. It was there and existed and she knew it and that was it. Since she need never leave the house again, she thought gratefully, she was not going to have to see supermarket eyes averted in recognition and shame. She was not going to have to see the tight, pained half-smiles of teachers. Pat would, though. He would probably revel in the sympathy; he seemed, she reflected, to like sympathy in direct inverse proportion to the loathing Beth felt for the same glances, notes, and little hand-hugs. He'd even said, one night, how heart-warming it was, how startling a confirmation of the basic good in human beings, the letters and the offers of support that caused the mail carrier literally to heft armfuls of stuff up onto their porch; it would never have fit in any mailbox. Laurie, Beth believed, took the letters home. She could see Laurie eye the growing piles nervously every time she came over, and then, a few days later, Beth would notice the piles were slim again. She could not imagine, nor did she try, what manner of pity and grotesquerie those letters contained.

On her bad days, after Kerry fell asleep on her bottle, Beth took baths. She sat in the water until it was scummy and cold, looking at her spindly arms and legs, white as carp, floating under the surface. By the time she came out, it was four or after, Jill was often home if it wasn't a late class day, and she'd gone to get Vincent at the Shores'. Beth could start waiting for dark. Deep dark came early now, and as soon as it was deep dark, a person could go to bed. Bed, for Beth, was a nearly erotic sensation. The falling away of the day was her most precious moment of existence. The nights when Jill had class were nearly intolerable. She had to sit on the couch while Vincent read his chapter books or went over his spelling lists, knowing she should get up and tell him that children did not do homework effectively in front of television, but unable to do it. After a while, he would get up, gingerly kiss her, and go to bed.

And then Beth would have the last fifteen minutes, the fifteen minutes to get through that she usually spent watching Paul Crane, across the street, doing endless chip shots on his frost-nipped lawn under the lights from his garage. After fifteen minutes — it was a reasonable interval — she could run for the stairs. Vincent would be in bed. She would even look in on him, blurring her eyes to avoid seeing the bed he lay in, and say, "'Night, honey." He never answered. He fell asleep quickly. That was good.

On good days, Beth sometimes went downstairs into her office and threw things away. She filled bags with out-take shots, old negatives and contracts, her clips, her anthologies, phone numbers she would never need again. She liked the feeling of stripping away her former life, liked the release from any obligation except living until night. One afternoon, Pat had discovered her throwing away her Rolodex and stopped her. Beth let him — she could always throw it away some other day, when he was at the restaurant.

She thought, briefly, of actually dismantling her darkroom, but she knew that she would never be able to dispose of huge stable objects such as sinks and trays without Pat's noticing. At night, she would mentally scan her own room, thinking of what things she could throw away the next day. Shoes, perhaps. She had far too many.

When Candy showed up on the porch that afternoon, Beth had had a good morning. She had showered and fed Kerry her cereal on her own. She let Candy come in, returned her hug, and felt puzzled by the way Candy held her at arm's length and looked her over, top to bottom.

"Beth, what you are wearing is very strange," Candy said.

Beth asked if Candy wanted coffee. Candy said, "Sure." And Beth went into the kitchen to measure out the coffee in spoons. Laurie always said it tasted better if you measured it.

"Did you hear me, what I said before?" Candy asked, when they were sitting at the kitchen table, Candy holding a drowsy Kerry in one arm.

"Yes," Beth said. She tried to remember.

"You are wearing something that looks funny." Beth was, in fact, wearing ordinary wool pants. They were pants from the seventies, which she had discovered not long ago during a closet raid. She had no idea how much weight she'd lost, but on impulse she had tried on these pre-childbearing pants, with their wide legs and eccentric wraparound belts, and found that they nearly fit. There had been perhaps three pairs, which Beth now wore regularly, with either one of her sweatshirts or one of Pat's shirts.

"I've lost a lot of weight," she told Candy. "And these are just fine for working around the house."

"What about for *working* working?" Candy asked then.

"I'm . . . uh . . . retired," Beth said. "I can't imagine . . . you know. I took pictures of news things and people and weddings and stuff, Candy. I couldn't do that now. I don't think I could take pictures of . . . food, even."

"But you might want to — you know, sometime," Candy said. "Don't you think? I mean, didn't you always work?"

Beth nodded.

"Oh," Candy said. "That's what I thought." She went on to tell Beth that the seminar she was attending was being held at the big new conference center west of town. "The Embassy's cheaper, though, so I'll get a room there." But Beth told her no, of course not, she must stay here, it would be fine. Candy smiled. "I'd like that." What the conference was about, she went on, was the psychological profiling of felons. "It's the big new thing," Candy explained. "You get to find out that almost every criminal is between twenty and forty, medium height, white or black, drank milk as a child, had a little trouble with alcohol in college, and had a mother who always bugged him to practice the piano."

"I think I dated that guy," Beth said.

"I think my brother was that guy," Candy agreed. "It's my belief that this is all bullshit, actually. I don't really think there are any more bad guys percentage-wise than there ever were. What I think is that there are simply more people, you know? There are more people, and

211

less room for them, and less money."

She was not mentioning Ben, Beth noticed. That would be because there was nothing new to say. Beth had learned not to ask. Candy would tell her anything, no matter how seemingly minute or insignificant. But attention was shifting away from the case. Beth knew that.

"Did you see the story in *People* last week?" she asked Candy then.

"I was hoping you didn't," Candy told her. "But actually, Bethie, much as I despise most of the sharks, I really think this isn't such a bad idea. It's like free leafleting. Every kid goes to a doctor's office sooner or later. It could be our key, you know? One of those reality TV shows would probably be a good idea, too." She paused, swirling the coffee gone cold in her cup. "You or Pat would probably have to chat, though."

Beth said, smiling, "No."

"No for you or no for Pat?"

"I'm not his mother. I don't care what he does."

"Oh, so that's how it is, huh?"

"I mean, I don't care who he talks to. He doesn't seem to do it much, anymore, though."

"Maybe he can sense you don't like it."

"Maybe."

"Beth — " Candy said then, and waved to Jill as she came in the door from school, handing her the baby, who woke up and kicked in delight, saying "Joo! Joo!" and gurgling. "Do you have any money?"

"Do you need some money?"

"No, I meant, do you have any money in the house? I thought we could go shopping."

Beth started to laugh. She thought she might laugh hard enough that the coffee would come up in brown strings, so she tried to keep it under some semblance of control. Everything, it seemed, made her stomach revolt in recent months. "Candy," she finally gasped. "I don't go shopping. What would I go shopping for?"

"Some clothes, maybe."

"I don't want any clothes."

"Would you do it for me?"

"No."

"That's not very hospitable. Maybe *I* want some clothes."

"You live in Chicago. They have much better clothes there than they have in Madison. Anyway, you always wear the same thing. And they have beige blazers anyplace."

"Beth, that's not true. I have a quite varied wardrobe at home. Leather studded with nails, mostly. Some gold lamé. What I want, I want to go shopping. Jilly," she called, "where's a good mall?"

Jill, changing the baby, called back, "West Towne. The Limited and stuff."

"Sounds good." Candy got up. At that moment Vincent opened the door. To Beth's astonishment, he flew into Candy's arms, holding her, wrapping his legs around her as she picked him up — easily, Beth noticed, fragile as Candy looked.

"Did you bring Ben?" he asked.

213

"Sport, not yet." Candy looked about to cry. "I'm sorry. I'm going to keep on looking till I find him, though. I promise. So, Vincent, school okay? Playing basketball?"

Vincent slid his eyes over toward his mother. "I'm not playing this winter."

"Oh, well, time enough for that. Listen, Vincent, I have a big problem."

"What?"

"I'm taking your mommy to the store, and I have to have someone to guard my badge while I'm gone." She took out the leather case that held her gold shield. "This is a detective's badge. It's very valuable." She winked at Beth. "It's real gold, for one thing. And it has powers. Do you have any idea of anybody who could guard this thing, I mean guard it with his life, while I'm gone?"

Vincent lowered his voice. "I think I could do it."

"I don't know." Candy pretended to back off a step. "I don't know, Vincent. You're a smart kid and all, but you're only what — eight? This is the kind of responsibility I wouldn't normally let even a kid, like, twelve do for me. It would have to be a very trustworthy kid."

"I am," said Vincent. "Ask Jill. I make my own bed."

"Well, Jill, what do you think?"

"I think the captain is up to the assignment," Jill said. "But you can't take it to Alex's or anything, big buddy."

"Can I ask him over and show it to him?"

Candy pondered, tapping her teeth. "Can this . . . Alex be trusted?"

"He's my best friend," Vincent confided.

"Well, then, yes. It's unorthodox procedure. But this once, okay." She turned to Beth. "If you haven't got any money, have you got some bank cards or something?"

"Yes, she does," Jill sang out. "They're in the envelope taped to the fridge. They won't recognize her signature, though. They only know mine. I'm Beth Cappadora now."

"Not today," Candy told her, palming the card. "Do you want to put on something . . . ? Well, it doesn't matter. Come on, Beth. Let's go."

The light off the snow was pitiless on Beth's eyes. Her ancient pea coat felt bulky — she hadn't been farther than the mailbox very often since fall. Even the motion of Candy's car was like a fresh sensation, something only vaguely familiar. "It's cold," she told Candy.

"It's January, Beth," Candy said. "It's traditionally cold in January."

"It's just that I haven't been . . . getting out much."

"So I see."

At the sight of the teeming mall — didn't people know Christmas was over? What did they find to buy, endlessly buy, forever? — Beth nearly begged for mercy. And people who read *People* might recognize her face. (Had her face been in the story? It had definitely been in some stories.) People would remember. They'd stare.

"I don't know, Candy," she said, trying to

sound just a little bored, restless. "It's so crowded in these joints."

"We'll only go to one store. I just don't know what one store. So bear with me."

They ended up at a place called Cotton to Cotton. "I like cotton," Candy said. "It never wrinkles, and if you put a lot of it on, you're as warm as if you were wearing wool. Layers, Bethie. That's the ticket."

And Beth was stunned; Candy was as good at clothes as she'd been at makeup that horrible night. After studying Beth's face in the relentless fluorescent overheads for a few long moments, Candy said, "Purple. Teal. Gray. Real blue. Maybe a little red." And she'd gone off for armloads of skirts and tunics and vests and belts, sweaters and jackets, which she'd draped over Beth as she stood, mute as a mannequin, in the middle of one of the aisles.

After forty minutes, Candy had filled four shopping bags, and Beth had surrendered her card. On the way home, she told Beth, "Now, the deal is, you can wear any one of those things with any other one of those things. So if one is dirty, just pull out another one and put it on. They all go together, even the belts. And you can wear black shoes with every single thing. Flats or heels. You do have black shoes, don't you?"

"Yes," said Beth.

"So you don't have to think about it. You just pull out whatever is there and you put it on. See? And when we get home, I'm going to hang them all in your closet for you, in

216

one place, and then we're going to take all the disco pants and ... make a bonfire or something. Okay?"

"Okay," Beth said.

The clothes still had the tags on them two months later when Laurie, who had called a dozen times, increasingly sorrowful, showed up one night as Pat was just about to head back to the restaurant. Beth, upstairs sitting on her bed, heard her ask Pat, "She still won't talk to me, will she?"

"I think she would," Pat replied. Beth could tell by the muffling of Pat's voice that he was giving Laurie a hug. "I think she's over it. I mean, Barbara Kelliher has called her a zillion times telling her how great the response was to the story, how she's had to have new posters made five times. I think she understands."

"I think she hates my guts," Laurie said. But Beth could hear her tripping up the stairs; even on this errand into Rochester's mad wife's room, Laurie was bouncy.

"Hi," she said.

"Hi," said Beth.

"What're you doing?"

"Curing cancer," Beth said. "I just put away my test tubes."

"Oh, well, good," Laurie said, sitting down on the bed. "Can you please just forgive me? Just get it over with? We are never going to agree on this, Bethie, but we've been friends for a thousand years, and you know, you have to admit that you know, I would never, ever do anything knowingly to harm you."

"I know that," Beth said.

"Good, because I have something I want you to do for me."

The nerve, Beth thought. But she asked, "What?"

"I want you to take a picture."

"I don't do it anymore."

"Just this once. There's a lot of dough in it. A lot."

"How much?" Pat asked, walking in.

Beth said, "I don't do it anymore."

"They'll come here."

"I don't do it."

"Just let me tell you." It was a wedding announcement picture, but the bride — the daughter of a client of Laurie's husband, Rick — couldn't go to a studio for the shot.

"Why? What's wrong with her?"

"Nothing. Except she's . . . very pregnant."

"Big deal."

"Well, Beth, her family are immigrants from China. To some people it still *is* a big deal. She's very modest."

"Not when it counted," Beth said, starting to feel like some evil old spider crouched in her den, which wasn't how she'd intended to appear at all.

Laurie sighed. "Anyhow, this girl's mom and dad are modest, and very rich. So I said I knew someone who could take the picture in a very private setting, and make it look . . . like she isn't. A real magician. You," Laurie said.

"You could do it, Bethie," Pat put in. "You

218

wouldn't have to go out."

"Take a picture of a pregnant woman? Me?" she sneered. Oh, Pat, if money had lips, we'd never have kissed, Beth thought. "You've got to be nuts."

"Please, Bethie, this once," Laurie pleaded. "Let me get over my guilt by doing you a good turn. If you hate it, just never do it again."

"This is not a good turn. This is a setup," Beth said. "Anyhow, I can't, because I threw out all my paper and stuff."

"I'll get you paper. I'll get you supplies," Pat offered eagerly.

Beth sighed, longingly thinking of her pills and the lure of her down comforter.

"When?" she asked.

★ ★ ★

It was an astounding thing, what happened. When they came, the boy chipper, the girl sullen, both their mothers glowering, Beth set them up as briskly as she would have arranged fruit on a plate. And when she began to shoot, she realized that this was exactly how she saw them. She remembered what a high-school art teacher had told her, one of those tiny, utterly basic things that transform a pattern of thought: that when most people see a cup on a table, they think of it as sitting flat, so they draw it sitting flat. In fact, she had told Beth, the bottom of the cup really looks curved, and that was the correct way for it to be rendered. "It's

219

the difference between seeing with your brain and seeing with your real eye," the teacher had explained.

And, for the first time in her professional life, Beth saw the couple as a series of angles and curves, planes and shadows, not as people with emotions and histories, people who had writhed in love and spat in disgust. She saw them not with her brain — her brain, she reasoned later, was gone — but with her photographer's eye alone. She lit them as she would have lit statues, as, in fact, she had lit statues and architectural pictures.

The portraits that resulted were stunning. The very, very wealthy father gave her a thousand dollars. Laurie turned up more subjects willing to come to Beth's lair. And by late spring, Beth grew willing to go out to them — to shoot pictures of people-as-things that both the subjects, and, later, publishers praised for their sensitivity and humanity. Even, after a while, children. They were just smaller apples and oranges in baskets.

The first time she had to travel to an assignment, she pulled out a skirt of deep lavender and a red tunic, tied it with a black sash, and slipped on a pair of black shoes. She looked skinny, still, eccentric, and . . . not bad. By the time summer came, Beth, looking back on several months of increasing business, realized she had found a key, thanks to Candy's wiles and Laurie's stubbornness — a way to fill hours and appear productive, without the need to feel or even think very much, not even about whether her belt matched her shoes. She sent Jill back to Cotton to Cotton for more hues and shapes when the first ones succumbed to washing. It worked.

Beth had found what passed for a life.

12

Vincent

October 1987

HIS mother said even she didn't know
what the square box built into the wall
on the staircase was supposed to be.
She told Vincent once that back when she and
Dad were kids, people liked to put telephones
in little nooks all over their houses. "This house
was probably built in the sixties. Maybe that's
what it was," she said.

"Why would anybody want a phone in the
middle of the stairs?" he had asked, eagerly.
But by then his mother was looking past him,
the way she did that made Vincent turn his
head to try to see the person she had spotted
somewhere just behind him. But there was never
anybody there.

Grandma Rosie told Vincent she thought the
people who originally owned Vincent's house
were good Catholics. "They would have a figure
of Our Lady in there, or Saint Anthony," she
had said last Christmas Eve, when she passed
Vincent crouched in the square den of a hole
on her way up to bed. "It is not for little boys
who are trying to stay awake all night so Santa
will pass by this house and leave no presents."
She took his hand and led him to bed.

Baby Kerry, who could talk now, called the box her 'baby house'. She took her dolls and her phony waffles and the syrup bottle that looked like it was really pouring in there, and he would pretend to be the customer while she pretended to sell him waffles. Or you could sit there, all tucked up, like Vincent imagined mice would feel in their holes, and see right down into a corner of the kitchen — the corner that had the sink and the Mister Coffee. And if the dishwasher wasn't on, you could hear everything anybody said down there.

That was how Vincent got to hear about how his mom was trying to kill his dad.

First, his dad put his hand on his mother's top, around one of her boobies, which he did a lot, and which Vincent thought usually meant his dad was trying to be nice — the way Grandpa Bill did when he messed up your hair. Vincent didn't like anyone to mess up his hair — he liked his hair just so, nice and flat and soft — but he knew that with Grandpa Bill, this hair-messing deal was like hugging. So he put up with it. That's what the boobie thing was, too. But his mom didn't like it any better than Vincent liked getting his hair ruffled. She pushed his father's hand away. Then his father kissed her. She smiled then, and looked down, down into the sink, as if she were trying to find a contact lens.

"Bethie," said Vincent's father. "Honey, we have to talk."

"I have to print," his mother said. "I have

223

four phone calls to make. I have to get Vincent ready for school."

"He isn't even up yet."

Ha-ha, Daddy, thought Vincent.

"Well, he should be."

Vincent's dad sighed. It was a big sigh, meant to get his mom to turn around and say, "Okay, what do you want?" But she didn't; she just kept on messing with the sink, and finally his father tried again:

"Dad wants an answer, Beth. He wants me to think about this seriously, and make a decision within the year."

"So make a decision within the year, Pat," said his mother.

"After all, Beth, this is what all this goddamn work I've put in was for . . . "

"Pat, I've heard all this — "

"This is what all the years I've spent at Cappadora's, and before that, filling cartons of potato salad at my dad's — "

"Pat, we've been over and over this." Watch it, Dad, Vincent thought.

That's the voice you don't want to hear, the voice that came right before Mom's fingers went like a lobster claw around your upper arm. Dad was pretty smart. He got up and put his arms around Mom again; he kissed her. She let him.

"Kiss, kiss, kiss," his dad said softly, almost as nice as if he was talking to one of the kids. "Don't we ever just fuck anymore?"

Vincent had heard his dad use the *f* word before, but not in such a nice voice. He leaned forward; they weren't looking up, so they weren't going to see him anyway.

"Pat," said his mother. "I have to get the baby up . . . " Kerry was not a baby anymore, she was going to be two, but everybody still called her that.

"We have time," said his dad.

"Okay. You go upstairs and get my diaphragm and fill it up with gunk, and then . . . let's see, we'll have about eight minutes before I have to get some food in Vincent before he gets on the bus . . . want to do it right here? I can make toast at the same time?"

"That's a lousy thing to say, Beth. It isn't like I'm on top of you every second. We have sex about as often as we pay the water bill."

"Talk about lousy things to say . . . "

"And anyway, I don't see why you need the gunk and the diaphragm every damn time."

"Because I don't want to get pregnant every damn time."

"Beth, that's another thing . . . "

Vincent's mom got quiet. His dad didn't get the message, though; he kept right on talking: "It's been well over a year, Bethie. We both know that Ben — "

"What's that got to do with it?"

"Jesus, Beth. Don't you give a damn about the way I hurt?" Vincent's dad started to go out into the hall; Vincent shrank back against the sides of the box. "I mean, Bethie, I was the guy who had three kids. Everybody thought I was nuts, you know? *Three* kids? But one of the worst things is, for me, that the house was so full of their noise before. I would want to run up the walk at lunch — "

Vincent's mom flashed across the lower hall so fast he barely saw her. She opened the front door. It was a thing she did a lot, just opening the front door and letting the air in, even if it was really cold. Just standing there, blowing out her breath.

"Pat, I don't want another child," she said.

"You said you would think this over."

"I *have* thought it over. And every time I think of having another child in me, and that maybe it would be a boy . . . " Her voice got funny, like she had a bread ball stuck. "Pat, it isn't going to change anything. Don't you see that? Just so you can be the guy who has three kids again."

"Not just that. I'm not a fool."

"No, I mean, it would just be numbers. It would be a compensatory child. Like a replacement part. Like getting a new gravy boat so you don't spoil the set."

"You're a bitch," said Vincent's dad.

"I have no doubt," said his mom, "that I'm a bitch. But the fact is, I'm not going to have a baby and I'm not going to move to Chicago so you can start a restaurant with your dad. If you want a new baby and a restaurant in Chicago, you need a new wife."

"Is it so wrong for me to want us to be a family again? Have a normal life again?"

"Pat. There is no such thing as having a normal life again."

Vincent heard the door bang shut, and he had the feeling his mom hadn't done it.

"There would be, if you even tried . . . "

"Pat," said his mom, and it was her being-nice voice, the voice she used to try to get him not to open the door when she had pictures in the bath and the red light was on. "Do you know what it's like for me?"

Vincent's dad said nothing.

"Do you?"

Nothing.

"It's like I'm always under this giant shelf of snow or rock, and if I move, if I change my position even a little, the snow is going to start to slide, and it's going to come down on me and bury me . . . "

"Oh, Beth . . . "

"No, it really is. I don't dare to think about him for a full minute. I don't dare to think about the reunion for a full minute. If I thought of having to live where I'd drive by the Tremont every day of my life . . . "

"We wouldn't have to."

"Pat, I hear you and Tree talking. You and Monica. We'd all be together again. In the old neighborhood. The kids under the table while the adults play poker. Just like the old days. Don't you think I know that Tree hates me for keeping you up here? Away from your parents, who want you so bad, so much more now that they're grieving? Don't you think I know that my own father thinks I should come home, where Bick can help me, because I'm such a mess?"

"Everybody hates you, Beth, right? Nobody understands how — "

"But if I move, Pat, if I move one inch, that

avalanche is going to come down on me and you'll have to raise these kids by yourself — "

"Which I already practically do."

"Okay, okay. I accept that. Pat's always been the good one. Pat's the rock. He's the one who's held that poor crazy woman and those little kids . . . like the *People* story, Pat. Didn't you love it? 'His hands sturdily on the backs of his wife and his remaining son.' You're such a hero, Pat."

"And you're such a martyr, Beth."

"I have to get Vincent up." Vincent got up onto his knees, ready to take off for Ben's bed and dive in if she moved. "But Pat, you know, you can't force me to do anything. You can't. You can't threaten me like when we were in college, because I don't give a damn if you leave, or . . . or . . . or if you screw every pizza waitress in Madison."

"What?"

"I mean, you don't have any power over me, Pat. The worst already happened."

"I love how you say 'it happened.' Like it was a tornado or something." There was such a stillness in the hall that Vincent could hear Kerry's mouth open in her sleep, with a tiny pop. Pretty soon she would come waddling down the hall, and that would be good, he was hungry, and they were going to fight . . . The sunlight spun the dust over and up, over and up. Vincent put out his hand to let it rest on his palm. They weren't done. He could wish all he wanted, but they weren't done, and he might not get breakfast at all.

"What do you mean by that?"

"Nothing," said Vincent's dad. It was his dad's lie voice, the voice he used when he said "I'm not tired," so Vincent knew something else was coming. "I mean nothing."

"You do. You mean it didn't just happen."

"It just happened. Forget it, Beth."

"No, you've been keeping it inside, and you want me to know that you blame me. Don't you think I already know that you blame me, because *you* would never have let Ben get lost, would you, Pat? You'd never have been such a bad, shitty parent, who only cared about herself — "

"I never once said that, Beth."

"Said it? You didn't have to say it. It was evident, Pat. That line around your mouth, Pat. You hate my guts, and you blame me for losing your son."

Vincent saw his dad blast out of the living room like he was going to grab his mother and knock her down.

"Okay, Beth! Do I blame you? Sure as shit I blame you! Candy blames you, and Bender does, too. So does Ellen. Don't you think everyone thinks that if you just had a minute to take care of your kids, none of this would ever have happened? Just because they don't tell you? Does a wall have to fall on you? Yeah, you were lucky all your life until now, Beth. You could do everything half-assed and get away with it, because I was there to clean up after you!"

"You piece of shit," said Vincent's mother. "You self-righteous — "

"I'm not self-righteous, Beth. I'm right! I'm just right! Kids don't just vanish like smoke, Beth. They don't 'get lost'. People lose them."

"I hate you, Pat," said Vincent's mother.

Vincent jumped up and ran down the hall into Kerry's room. His head was hot like he had a fever. He raced over to the baby's crib and let down the bar and, reaching up, clamped his whole hand over her little nose and mouth. He didn't want to kill her . . . he loved Kerry. She was struggling now, trying to get his hand away, trying to breathe, her big gray eyes scared, bubbling tears . . . Vincent didn't know if he could let go yet, but finally Kerry twisted her head just right and opened her getting-blue lips and began to scream, not a baby-wet cry (Vincent knew the sniffly-wheezy quality of that; he'd heard it a million times, first with Ben) but a horror-movie scream, like a big girl's . . . and Vincent's mom was up the stairs like she had wings, knocking him to one side as she pulled Kerry out of the crib (Kerry's lips were starting to get pink again), screaming, "What did you do to her? Vincent, answer me! What did you do to Kerry?"

His dad was right behind his mom, and he grabbed Kerry out of her arms, and they held her between them, his dad saying, "Beth, she's okay — remember, the doctor always says if they're crying, then they're okay . . . It looks like she lost her breath for a minute . . . "

Then, his mom was crying, holding Kerry in her arms, and his dad tried to pull his mom against him, but she shoved him away, harder even than she'd shoved Vincent. His dad grabbed Vincent's arm and pulled him off the floor. "Get your sweatshirt on," he said. "We're going for a ride."

"He has school!" his mom screamed.

"Not today!" his dad yelled back.

"Where are you taking him?"

"Somewhere safe, Beth! Safe from you! You're going to kill me off sooner or later, but not him!" And Vincent was practically lifted off his feet as his father skimmed him, with his sweatshirt only one arm on, down the stairs and out into the garage.

"Daddy," Vincent said, "wait a minute. I got to get my vitamin."

"I'll wait in the car," his dad said, fumbling for a cigarette in his shirt pocket.

Vincent ran back into the house — good, she was still up in Kerry's room; he could hear her humming and crying, the floorboards squeaking as she walked Kerry back and forth. Working quickly, Vincent went first into his dad's office, where he set the alarm for 11:00 p.m. Then into their bedroom (he had to pass Kerry's door for it, but the door was shut, so that was okay), where he changed the alarm setting from 6:30 to 4:30 in the morning. And then, he couldn't think, yes . . . okay, the stove timer. He could barely reach it. He set that for 5:00 a.m. Maybe that wasn't all the alarms in the house, but that was all he could think of so fast. She would notice, for sure. He could stand right next to her face while she slept, he could even put out his finger and touch her eyelid, and she

231

wouldn't ever wake up. He'd called her a dozen times, when he had his running-away dreams, but she'd never wake up, though sometimes his dad did, if he called more than once. She would notice this, and he wouldn't care even if they did come back tonight, which he had a feeling they weren't going to, because his dad had grabbed his little bag with his toothbrush and shaver in it. He wouldn't care if the alarms woke him up, too. Or even Kerry, though this wasn't her fault.

Vincent snatched an orange Flintstones out of the bottle on the sink and jumped into the front seat of the car. "Belt," said his dad, staring ahead, and Vincent snapped it on and sat back. They went down the belt line, past the turnoff on Park Street for Cappadora's, past the road that led to Rob Maltese's, his dad's best friend's, house. Past the car wash. To the Janesville exit, the sign that his father once said meant, "We're going to see Grandma!"

"Are we going to Chicago?" Vincent asked.

"Don't you want to go see Grandma Rosie?"

"It's a school day, Daddy. It's not Sunday or Friday even."

"Sometimes, we could go see Grandma Rosie even in the middle of the week, like in summer."

"But why?"

"Just to see her. Don't you ever want to see your mama? I just want to see my mama," his father said, in a little-bitty voice that scared Vincent much more than the *f* word or any of the yelling in the hall. Pat lit a cigarette and rolled down the window. "Don't tell Mommy I smoked in the car," he said, like he always said.

"I won't."

"Okay, pal."

Vincent leaned against the arm rest; his father was singing with the Rolling Stones on the radio, using the heels of his palms like drums; Vincent thought he might fall asleep, if he wasn't afraid of the running-away dream, the dream which wasn't so scary in itself as the way his dream self kept wanting to look behind him. He knew that if he looked behind him, it would be the worst thing, worse than the flabby white monster with the big red mouth he saw by accident one time when he got up and his dad had *Shock Theater* on in the middle of the night.

It would be worse than that, Vincent thought; he wanted to tell his dad that, but his eyes were blurry.

"Wake up," said a voice, a voice that always sounded like it had a cough in it, or stones under it. Grandpa Angelo. "Wake up, *dormi*-head." That was the Italian word for 'sleepy', part of the song Grandpa Angelo sang when Ben was little. Vincent was sweaty and shivery, but he put his arms up and Grandpa Angelo lifted him out through the window of the car and held him against the rough wool of his blue suit. Grandpa Angelo wore blue suits all the time, even on Saturday morning in the house, even when he went to get a fireplace log or spray the tomatoes. Grandma Rosie said wearing the blue suit all day made Grandpa look like an immigrant, but he told her, "Rose, a businessman has a big car and a clean suit. Not just at business — all day long." Except

233

playing cards. When Grandpa Angelo used to play cards with his friends — Ross, Mario, and Stuey — he wore his stripey cotton T-shirt with straps over the shoulders. You could see the tufts of white hair stick up from Grandpa's shoulders over the straps, like feathers. If he saw Vincent, he would pull him down on his lap and rub his cigar cheek against Vincent's, and put red wine from his good glass on his finger and let Vincent lick it off. He would ask Vincent, "Now, Maestro, do I ask this most illustrious dealer for one card, or two?" And even back then Vincent was not so little he couldn't tell when the red or black numbers had a gap in them — and he would shake his head no, because Grandpa told him the time to draw to an inside straight was never, ever, never; it was madness and doom. Sometimes, when the weather was hot and the locusts were caroling loud, Vincent would even fall asleep under Grandpa Angelo's white iron patio chair, the chorus of locusts and the slap of the cards and the sound of Italian swears and the hot, almost too sweet smell of cigars all wound around and around him until they seemed like one thing. And he would wake up shivery and sweaty, the sky changed from sunny to sunsetty, or from fresh to shiny overhead, just like it was now.

"My little love," said Grandpa Angelo. "My best boy." He carried Vincent up onto the front stoop, under the cool shade of the big green awnings. Vincent was deeply fond of the awnings, the only ones on the block, and of the shiny green, absolutely square hedges that looked like plastic but smelled like vinegar.

"I love you, Grandpa," Vincent told him, nuzzling. And he did, too. He also loved his grandpa Bill, but his grandpa Bill always seemed to be a little nervous around Vincent. Like he would ask him, "Hey, Vince, you married yet?" Like a nine-year-old kid would be married and not even tell his own grandfather. Grandpa Angelo just gave you penne and red sauce, or white sauce if your tummy was upset, and wine from a spoon and Hershey's kisses from his pockets, and let you pick the grapes and tomatoes and only laughed if you dropped one — and not a phony, grown-up, really-mad-behind-it laugh, either. He really didn't care what a kid did as long as a kid said his pleases and thank-yous and didn't be a *diavolo* — Vincent didn't know exactly what that meant but knew it was a bad guy.

They were passing the kitchen, going outside to the backyard, when Vincent heard his dad say, " . . . what else to do, Ma. I can't take anymore."

"Patrick, *tesoro mio*," said Grandma Rosie, who was getting his dad coffee. "She's not herself. You must give her time."

"I have no more time, Ma!" Vincent realized, to his terror, that his dad was crying. "I want to have a life, Ma, not this . . . prison on Post Road that Beth never goes out of — I mean, not willingly, just up and down to her darkroom . . . Ma, I want out of this!"

Grandma Rosie swiveled her head around, fast, and then said in a big voice, meant for Vincent's dad, too, "Vincenzo, *carissimo*! Grandma will come and see you in a minute."

Grandpa Angelo carried Vincent outside, set him down in one of the white iron chairs, and brought him a glass of orange juice. "In a little while, we'll have pasta, eh? But first, we give your daddy some time with Grandma."

"Daddy's crying," said Vincent.

"He's so sad, 'Cenzo," said Grandpa Angelo, sitting himself down heavily in the chair opposite. He started flicking through the tapes on his bench, next to his big tape player. "We must have some music now, eh?"

"Why?"

"Good for the soul!" said Grandpa.

"No — Daddy. Why's he sad?"

"He's sad because of your brother, dear one. He's missing Ben."

"And he hates my mommy. She said."

"No, Vincenzo, your daddy loves your mommy. He loves her since he was a little boy like you. She's his best buddy."

"I think Rob is his best buddy."

"Well, she's his best buddy and his true love. It's just . . . here!" said Grandpa, finding a tape. "It's just she's so sad and he's so sad, they forget their love."

"Mom forgot my school conference three times. The principal had to call. And then Dad went."

"Well, you see then. This is so hard a time for us. For me, too. I think of my Ben and it crushes my heart." He patted his leg and

236